Strange Beauty

Lori Weber

James Lorimer & Company Ltd., Publishers
Toronto

James Lorimer & Company Ltd. acknowledges the support of the Ontario Arts Council. We acknowledge the support of the Government of Canada through the Book Publishing Industry Development Program (BPIDP) for our publishing activities. We acknowledge the support of the Canada Council for the Arts for our publishing program. We acknowledge the support of the Government of Ontario through the Ontario Media Development Corporation's Ontario Book Initiative.

Cover design: Clarke MacDonald

Library and Archives Canada Cataloguing in Publication

Weber, Lori, 1959-
     Strange beauty / Lori Weber.

(SideStreets)
978-1-55028-944-2 (bound).— 978-1-55028-941-1 (pbk.)

     I. Title. II. Series
PS8645.E24S73 2006   jC813'.6   C2006-903650-0

James Lorimer &
Company Ltd., Publishers
317 Adelaide St. W., Suite 1002
Toronto, Ontario
M5V 1P9
www.lorimer.ca

Distributed in the
U.S. by:
Orca Book Publishers
P.O. Box 468
Custer, WA USA
98240-0468

Printed and bound in Canada

For Lillian and Maria,
two beautifully strange and
strangely beautiful grandmothers,
who inspired me in many ways.

Chapter 1

Cindy is playing the mirror game — again. We're in the small bathroom on the third floor of the school, the one with only two stalls and one sink. Cindy's hogging that sink, with all her stuff spread around her on the counter — mascara, eye shadow, lipstick, hairbrush.

Beauty is important to Cindy.

"Hurry up, Cindy. We'll be late for class," I say from my post at the door, behind the green tiled wall.

"So. Who cares?" she calls back.

"I do," I say. Lately, Cindy has been making me feel pathetic for caring about what teachers think. She thinks I should care more about my looks, but I could never stand in front of a mirror for half an hour. I wouldn't know what to do. In the mornings, I usually get washed and brush my long, brown hair. Sometimes I'll pull it back, if it looks dirty. But I don't wear makeup. My eyes are dark, like my hair, and I have long eyelashes. Once, I tried wearing eyeliner and mascara to school, and by the end of the day I had black marks all around my eyes, like spider tracks. I think I look fine without all that stuff.

"Oh my God, he's coming," says Sharon. She is also standing guard at the door. If Min were at school today, she'd be here too, standing further down the hallway, like an early warning system. But today it's just the two of us, one looking down the hallway, one looking up.

Sharon flies around the corner into the bathroom, calling out, "Ding ding!"

"Crap!" Cindy says, throwing her makeup into her bag. I can hear plastic colliding with plastic. This is what she's been doing her face for — to impress Jason. As if she really needs to try. His tongue practically falls to the floor whenever he sees her, like every other guy's. Cindy's looks really changed over the summer. She grew a couple of inches, and let her hair grow to her waist. Even her boobs got bigger, way bigger than ours. She was always kind of the leader of our pack, on account of her personality, but now she's the leader on account of how she looks, too. Anyone who didn't know us would think she's at least a year older.

I'm supposed to go "dong" when I see Jason. That's our secret code. Sharon's ding and I'm dong. Min can be either. We've been walking doorbells since school started three weeks ago and Cindy suddenly developed this massive crush on Jason, who's in grade ten. Cindy wouldn't even have tried last year, but she jumped into grade nine determined to get a boyfriend, so why not go for an older boy? At least that's how she put it.

I hear Cindy ask Sharon how she looks. Sharon tells her she looks fantastic — as if Sharon would ever say anything different — at the exact same moment Jason veers off into the stairwell.

Ha! I think to myself. *Ding dong dell, Jason's in the well! Cindy's going to be mad as hell!*

Cindy steps out of the bathroom, flipping back her sandy-blond hair, her trademark gesture, a wide smile showing off her perfectly straight, white teeth. She's completely poised, ready to be captured by Jason's adoring eyes, or any other pair of eyes for that matter. It's like she can turn it on whenever she thinks someone is watching her. This summer, Cindy just happened to be at a Montreal Impact soccer game when the crowd was filmed for a commercial promoting the team. The camera lingered on her face for a second. For the rest of the summer, whenever that ad came on, Cindy would sit right next to the TV screen and point to herself. She said she was glad the camera had captured the mole over her lip, the one she thinks makes her look like Cindy Crawford.

"Where is he?" Cindy asks, scanning the hallway.

"He turned down the stairs," I respond. "Now can we go to class?"

"Penny! Why didn't you tell me?" Cindy glares at me. Her smile is gone, and her plump lips are set really hard, like a terrier's. I wonder what Jason would think if he saw her now.

"Sorry. What was I supposed to do? Run after him and drag him back?"

"Oh forget it, you wouldn't understand." Cindy waves me away, as if I'm an annoying kid, and takes off toward class, leaving me and Sharon to follow. Sharon has to take two steps for my every one, because her legs are so short. Neither of us speaks.

I resolve never to "dong" again. Every time I do it I feel like a human alarm system, like I should have wires and red flashing lights attached to my skin. And deep inside, I wonder why I ever agreed to do it. Sure, Cindy's been my best friend since grade two, when she first moved to my street, but that's not a good enough reason to go around donging. I think it has something to do with Cindy and who she is. Somehow, I've always felt luckier than her, on account of her family. She doesn't know her father, and her mother is pretty tough. She used to bring Cindy to school early and leave her alone in the schoolyard before the teachers were even on duty. Cindy would sit on the steps, staring at the other kids as they arrived. It meant she was always first in line to go in, but her hands would be blue from standing outside wearing nothing but thin gloves for so long. In grade two, the teacher sat me beside her and we ended up doing a lot of projects together. Cindy always took charge. She'd have the whole project — an animal poster, model igloo, whatever — all planned out. All I had to do was follow along. My family had to buy the supplies though — the glitter glue, cotton batten, and Popsicle sticks and whatnot. We never talked about it, but it always happened that way.

Eventually, because she lives across the street from me, Cindy's mother began bringing her over to our house early and we'd walk to school together with my grandmother. Cindy's mother always patted the top of her head before heading to work downtown, where she cleaned offices, and said, "Hang tough, kid." Sometimes, my grandmother would sneak cookies or muffins into Cindy's lunch bag. But Cindy never looked happy biting into the treats. She had a sour expression on her face, as though my grandmother's baking tasted bad.

Speaking of my grandmother, she would be horrified if she ever found out about this dingdonging business. "Never let anyone push you around," she often tells me. "You've got to know your own mind and stick to it." Then she'll launch into a whole thing about what life was like for girls when she was my age — no opportunity for anything other than housework and motherhood, etc. etc. "Complete subservience," she calls it.

Every time I dong, I feel like I'm letting her down.

Chapter 2

Cindy's in a bad mood for the rest of the day, just because Jason vanished. I can see her looking around for him outside after school, flipping her hair. Sharon is keeping an eye out, too, from the top of the front stairs. All she needs is a telescope. She loves to be the first to spot Jason. She'll whisper an enthusiastic "ding" into Cindy's ear whenever she does. Poor Sharon. She loves to be the first, the fastest, the loudest. I think it's on account of her illness. Sharon has some strange disease with a name that's ten syllables long. It's stunting her growth. In fact, she may never grow taller than she is now.

"You guys coming over?" I ask. It's kind of a ritual, hanging out at my place after school. I'm the only one whose parents aren't home, which means we can basically do what we want. My grandmother's there, but she's all right. She often bakes something, and she doesn't nag about homework.

"Sure," says Sharon. Cindy just nods. She's finally given up on running into Jason today.

We walk home up the back lanes, like we usually do. We hardly ever use the streets. There are no cars in the lanes, so we can do whatever we want. When we were younger, the four of us would link arms and try to walk the whole way home without breaking the chain. We didn't even separate for puddles or garbage cans. Most of the lanes are paved, except for one or two that are still dirt and gravel, which we avoid when it rains. They're also full of neat hiding places, like the wooden sheds that hold the fire escapes of the older triplexes, or under back stairs or bushes. We spent hours there playing hide and seek, or hiding objects that we'd give each other clues to find, when we were little.

"Should we throw something at the Queen's window, just for old time's sake?" asks Sharon, as we approach the dilapidated house at the end of our street. An old woman known as the Queen of Sheba lives there. She doesn't come out of her house often, but when she does, we can see that she has long grey hair with streaks of red. She dresses in black skirts and colourful shirts that billow around her tall frame when she walks. I've only seen her walking the streets a handful of times in my whole life. She usually only comes outside to feed the chickens she keeps in her backyard. The kids in our neighbourhood think she's a witch who catches children and boils them down for chicken feed. Just a few years ago, we were part of a gang who threw stones against her windows and whipped snowballs at her house in the winter. Anything to try to get a glimpse of her through the dusty glass.

"Sharon, when are you going to grow up?" Cindy snaps. *Ouch*! That must have stung. Even Cindy is normally careful about mentioning growing around Sharon.

"*Cindy*," I hiss at her.

"Sorry, Sharon," Cindy says a few seconds later, softening into her old self, the Cindy I remember becoming best friends with, before Diva-Cindy started to emerge.

"Hey, remember our trick with the bread?" Cindy says, laughing. She hunches over and slaps her knee, forgetting about perfect posture for a minute. "That was so awesome."

"Yeah, right. That's 'cause you were up in the tree keeping watch, while we were down on the ground risking our lives," I say. It had been Sharon's idea, of course. I remember her running excitedly into my backyard.

"We each have to go back home and sneak out some bread and string," she'd said. "You see, you tie the bread to the string, then attach it to a stick that you dangle near the chickens ..." As Sharon talked, Min shook her head gently. We'd have to get much closer to the Queen's backyard than usual. We had called to her chickens from a safe distance, clucking our tongues on the roofs of our mouths, but we'd never actually tried to touch them.

"Then we just wait," Sharon said. You see, *if* the chickens bite the bait, we have them. They'll strangle themselves."

And so we did it. And it nearly worked.

"You guys thought it was so funny, but I nearly died when that brown chicken started pecking at my piece of bread. Its ripply neck was so gross. I was petrified," I say.

"Yeah, but lucky for you I saw the Queen stick her ugly face out the door and saved your life," says Cindy. "Lucky for you I can whistle loud." She could, too. That's why she often got the look-out position high up in the tree.

Even the Queen's house is different. The buildings we live in are three-storey triplexes that run right around the block, without any space between them. But the Queen's house is a separate wooden one that sags in the middle, as if it's being pushed down by an invisible hand. The bushes that grow around it are tangled and snarled, like they've never been cut. When we were kids, we thought they were booby-trapped to catch us if we got too close.

Today we hurry past, the way we always do.

"Remember guys. Don't talk about the Queen in front of my grandmother. You know how she gets," I warn them. The way people treat the Queen of Sheba has always bothered Gran.

"She deserves just as much respect as anyone else," my grandmother always says. It's like she's got this radar for sensing when kids have been pestering the Queen, or even just thinking about it.

"Hi, kids," she says in the kitchen. "What fascinating things did you learn at school today?"

"Not much," I say, "the usual."

"Yeah, meaning nothing," Cindy says with a sigh.

"You kids should appreciate the advantages you have. You know I never went past grade four 'cause my parents couldn't afford to send me. I used to dream about going to school all the time. I wanted to go all the way, right to the top, Ph.D. and all. I used to picture myself in a black cap and gown at a big graduation ceremony. We all did. My whole generation, all of us were deprived, especially the girls. And look at you kids now ..."

"Gran! Okay. Enough. We appreciate school, right guys?" I look at my friends, widening my eyes so they get the message to keep quiet.

We get ourselves drinks from the fridge, then Sharon and I dig into the heap of still-warm cookies. My grandmother sits across from us, peeling potatoes for supper. She has pulled her white hair into a ponytail. I like the way she doesn't get her hair permed and frosted, like many old women do. Sometimes she'll let me braid her hair, or put it in pigtails. She's not afraid to wear it outside like that either. And I know she's given up wearing bras, which my mother doesn't approve of. My

16

grandmother says she's spent enough of her life following rules, in one way or another. At her age she just wants to be free, even if her boobs do slap against her tummy.

"Can you believe all the math homework Mr. Jackson's laying on us lately? All that Pythagorean crap. I'm drowning in it," Sharon says. "My mom says she's going to call the school." Sharon's mother would, too. She's really protective of Sharon. She seems to think all homework is a form of punishment.

"I know. Like, doesn't he know we have better things to think about?" Cindy says, rolling her eyes. Cindy's mother never gets too involved in her school stuff. She never finished high school herself. She had Cindy when she was only sixteen. Cindy's father was married to someone else at the time. That's just about all Cindy knows about him. She never sees him, but every year, on her birthday, he sends her a card with a cheque in it. She gets really excited about the money and always spends it on things her mother could never buy her, like CDs, an MP3, or expensive clothes.

I've often wondered how he signs his cards. 'Love, Dad' would be ridiculous, considering Cindy wouldn't even recognize him walking down the street. Could he really love someone he doesn't know?

I assume that Jason is the better thing that Cindy has to think about. What else could it be? He's all she wants to talk about. Right now, her head is down and she's picking at the skin around her nails like she doesn't want to talk, which is fine by me. It's not like I want to hear more about how gorgeous he is.

"These cookies are amazing," says Sharon, taking another one.

"Thank you, dear," my grandmother says. "What about you, Cindy? Not hungry?"

"Not really," Cindy says, without looking up.

"What a shame. You need to put on some weight. You all do," my grandmother says, getting up. She places the peeled-and-cut potatoes in a bowl of cold water and leaves the kitchen.

"Old people think everyone's too skinny," Cindy says. "If they had their way, we'd all be fat."

"A few cookies aren't going to kill us," I say. I'm on my third. The melted chocolate is running down my fingers.

"Speak for yourself. I need to be careful," Cindy says. "If I'm not, I'll turn into a cow."

"Cindy, you'd have to eat our whole fridge three times over to even begin to look like a cow."

"Yeah, well, whatever. I've got to go anyways. I'll see you guys."

Cindy picks up her knapsack and leaves. Cindy's mother expects her to have supper started by the time she gets home at five. In fact, Cindy's got a long list of chores to do around the house, like vacuuming and washing the bathroom, stuff I don't do. I've never actually seen

Cindy cleaning — I don't go to her house much — and I find it hard to picture. I guess she puts her hair up and uses rubber gloves, to protect her perfect nails.

"I'm going to save some of these for Min, in case she's better tomorrow," I say. Min's been home sick with the flu.

As I'm wrapping the cookies in a napkin, I think about Cindy. It's the first time I've ever seen her turn down my grandmother's cookies. Come to think of it, she's been acting funny about food lately. The four of us used to routinely pig out on a big bag of chips after school, but now Cindy just has one or two bites.

Sometimes, I think I can feel her using every ounce of her willpower not to take another bite.

Chapter 3

The next day, Ms. Melinowski, our history teacher, assigns a term project where we have to uncover an interesting piece of our own family history. We have to compile a fact sheet on the time and place, find pictures, and write a creative story. The whole thing is going to be presented to the class in a month.

"I want you all to see that history isn't just old names and dates, but actually part of the present," she says. "Your project should be something that really knocks our socks off."

"Can it knock our underwear off too?" one of the guys in the back calls out. Ms. Melinowski, who's a new teacher, blushes. Big mistake. She might as well paint a target on her forehead. She'll be easy prey for the rest of the year.

I smile at her on the way out and whisper, so that only she'll hear, "It sounds like a fun project,

Miss." It's like I've just rescued a drowning kitten, she looks so relieved.

"Thanks," she whispers back.

"What did you say to her?" Cindy asks. "I hope you told her we aren't interested in any ancient family history. Like, what exciting thing could possibly have happened to any of my relatives? Ooo, my great-great-grandfather had an ingrown toenail. Stop the press!"

"No. Actually, I told her it was a neat idea," I say. I wonder if Cindy even knows any of her grandparents. She never mentions them.

"You're kidding?"

I'm about to defend myself when Sharon cuts in. "Cindy. Ding! Ding!" We turn to see Jason walking towards us. I don't see why Cindy thinks he's so hot anyway. Sure, he's tall and dark, and has those blue eyes. But he carries himself as if he knows it, with a permanent smirk on his face.

When he gets close to us he stops and mouths hello to Cindy. She waves back at him. Then he hooks his finger to call her over.

Cindy walks across the hall as slowly as she can, so he has longer to take her in. It's like she's on a modelling runway. She even pivots a little when she's close to him.

They stand in a little huddle, talking and laughing, until the lunch bell rings.

"What did he want?" asks Sharon, when Cindy returns to us.

"Oh, he was just flirting, the way guys do. You know," Cindy says.

She knows that neither of us do know. Not first-hand at least. I wonder how Cindy suddenly learned her moves. Do some people just instinctively know how to flirt, or is it something everyone needs to learn? When I watch Cindy, I have the feeling she's copying something she's seen on television, like a commercial where two people fall all over each other, brought together by some ridiculous product, like air fresheners or toilet paper.

That night, at home, I think about my history project. I hate to admit it, but Cindy had a point about the odds of uncovering something juicy. My parents aren't exactly what you'd call exciting.

I walk into the kitchen, where my mother is ironing the clothes she and my father will wear to work tomorrow. Shirts, pants, and a skirt are suspended on hangers hooked over the backs of chairs and cupboard doors. My mother and father work in the same bank. That's how they met. They accidentally got locked in the vault one day, soon after they both started there. They were in it over one whole lunch hour, stuck behind the heavy iron doors. My friends think this story is romantic, but knowing my parents, they probably spent the hour taking inventory of the money.

"Mom," I say. She turns down the volume on her radio. She likes to listen to talk shows on professional topics, like "How to dress for success," and, "How to speak like you mean it."

"Is there any deep, dark mystery in our family's past? You know, like a murder-suicide or a two-headed baby? Something I could write about."

"Penelope?" My mother screws up her eyes. "You know there isn't. Why?"

"No reason. Forget it, Mom," I say. I wave my hand toward the radio, indicating she should get back to listening.

I find my father in his reclining chair in the living room, reading the *Financial Post*. My brother, Adam, is sprawled on the floor at his feet, sorting his Dinky car collection into piles. When he came home a few minutes ago, he had a very mischievous look on his face, and I caught him stuffing a few rocks that were still in his hand into his pockets. I bet he and his friends were pestering the Queen of Sheba, pelting her back door or something.

"Hey, Dad. Do you know any amazing or unusual family tales?"

"Umm …" my father pretends to think for a few seconds. "No, I don't," he says.

"No escapes from prisons, hiding out in caves in the mountains during wartime, that kind of thing."

"Ah, that would be cool," says Adam, inspecting a tiny ambulance.

"I'm afraid not, Penny. A bit too much normalcy in this family, I guess," my father says.

I bet this is easier for all those kids in my class whose families haven't lived in Canada as long as mine. We're third- and fourth-generation Canadians on all sides. And way back we came from ordinary places like England and Ireland. I hate to say it, but it does make us kind of bland — the white-bread family. Totally nuclear, two kids — one boy and one girl. The only thing we don't have to complete the picture is a dog, because my dad's allergic. Min will have an easy time with it. Her family stowed away in ships and made their way first to Europe, then to Canada, as refugees. Her grandfather was imprisoned in China during the Cultural Revolution just for writing poetry, which seems pretty warped.

"Thanks anyway, Dad," I say. But he has already flipped open the newspaper and is holding it like a shield in front of his face.

I knock softly on my grandmother's door. She was really tired after supper and went to lie down. She's been doing that a lot lately, but I guess it's not unusual to be tired when you're eighty-five!

"Come in," she calls.

"Hey, Gran. I need an interesting family story to write about. Do you know any?"

"Oh, good heavens, I know several. What kind do you want? Love, death, betrayal, prejudice, loyalty, murder?"

"Murder?"

"Well, you know my brother Johnnie was killed in a Japanese prisoner-of-war camp. That's murder, isn't it?"

"I guess so. What about the prejudice story?"

"Well, my sister Violet fell in love with a Mohawk man from Kanawakhe. My family was mortified and they forbade her to see him. That was back in the days when kids listened to their parents on matters like this. Poor Violet … she died a spinster, never married. She really loved him."

"Wow! That's so sad. What story do you know about loyalty?"

"It is very old story, full of a bit of everything really — love, hardship — all kinds of stuff."

"Tell me."

"I'll tell you tomorrow, Penny, when I'm rested."

"Oh, okay. It's just that I wanted to start working on it tonight. You can't tell me anything?"

"Well, sweetie, fire up that computer of yours and see what you can find on gypsies."

"Gypsies!"

"Good night, Penelope."

I settle into my chair and fire up my computer. I punch the word "gypsy" into Google. Two million, nine hundred and fifty thousand sites pop up. It would take me a year to look at all of these. I check Wikipedia. The first thing I learn is that gypsies are officially called "the Roma" and that they originated in northern India. And they sure have suffered a lot. I can't believe it was legal for Christians to kill gypsies in the Middle Ages. On another website there's a really crazy story about forty-five Roma who were executed in the 1700s for murdering some Hungarians. But those same Hungarians, who were supposedly dead, were there among the crowd, watching the execution. Some of the sites that I find have great pictures of gypsies, at different times and places, right up to today, living in tin shacks on the outskirts of big European cities, like Sarajevo and Budapest.

I go to bed wondering what my grandmother could possibly know about people who live so differently than we do.

Chapter 4

It's Saturday. My parents have taken Adam out to buy new hockey equipment, and I'm finally alone with my grandmother. I tell her some of the stuff I learned about gypsies last night.

"Did you know there are still twelve million gypsies living around the world, Gran?" I ask, hoping it will prompt her to tell me the story.

"Is that right, Penny? That's an awful lot, isn't it?"

"Well … are you going to tell me or not?"

"My story will mean a lot more to you if you know some background first. When I first met this person, I knew nothing at all about gypsies."

"So, it's about someone you actually know."

"Of course, Penny. You said you needed a family story for your project, didn't you?"

"We have a gypsy in our family?"

My grandmother laughs. "Good heavens, no.

Listen, why don't you do some more research while I get a few things done. Then I promise I'll tell you, later today. Okay?"

It's not okay. I'm dying of curiosity, but what can I do? I go back online and read some more about gypsies. I never knew they had such a fascinating history. If I do end up writing this story, I'm going to use this picture for my cover. It's of a girl who looks about the same age as me. She's wearing a long purple-and-red dress, with scarves tied around her waist. She's dancing, and the camera has caught her in the middle of a twirl, her hip sticking jauntily out to the side, her arms over her head, one hand holding a tambourine. Little kids dressed something like her are sitting on tree stumps, clapping their hands. A bright red caravan lies under a canopy of trees, its wooden steps pulled down, an old man and woman sitting on them. The woman's bosom is so big it spills onto her lap. Maybe they are the girl's parents.

I download a copy, in case I need it later, and continue reading. About an hour later, someone knocks at my door.

"Penny? Are you doing anything important? I want to take you somewhere." It's my grandmother. She hasn't taken me on an outing in ages, but we used to do it all the time when I was younger.

"Where are we going?" I ask her a few minutes later, as we head up our street.

"You'll see," she says. "If I'm going to tell you

this story, I might as well show you a thing or two."

I can't believe there are still things my grandmother knows that she hasn't told me about or shown me yet.

"You see these marks in the concrete?" Gran asks as we cross Jean Talon. I look down, but I don't see anything.

"Don't you see the faint metal rim? There's an old streetcar track under all those layers of concrete."

"I don't see a thing," I say.

"Ah, that's 'cause you don't know it's there. But I do, so I see it."

My grandmother once showed me an old five-cent streetcar ticket from her toffee tin at home. I tried to imagine what it must have been like to jump aboard a streetcar, clutching one of the wooden poles and twisting gracefully into a seat, pulling my long dress behind me. By the time my gran was born in 1915, women were no longer wearing really long dresses, but when my great-grandmother rode the streetcars, she would have.

"You know, my mother even rode the Rocket."

"The what?"

"The Rocket. The first electric streetcar in Montreal. She was just a little girl, sometime in the late '90s, 1890s that is, but she remembered it all her life." My grandmother's a walking encyclopedia when it comes to this city. "Although she always said she preferred the horses. All the kids did."

We step into the Park Avenue metro station, which is built into the old CP train station. We have to walk past a group of protestors who are carrying placards that say, "Save the station, Save History," and, "L'histoire, c'est nous!" I heard about it on the news the other night. Some big company wants to demolish the building and put in a supersize grocery store. They promised to keep the façade and the character of the building. "Character fiddlesticks" my grandmother said that night, sitting beside me. "How can a grocery store have character?"

"People just don't respect old things," she says now, sticking her ticket into the metal slot and pushing her way through the turnstile. "And speaking of old things, Penelope, today I'm going to show you my old neighbourhood, where I grew up."

"Wow, that's awesome." She's been telling me stories about her old neighbourhood for years, but has never taken me there.

"I haven't been back there for ages myself, Penny, so this will be an adventure for both of us."

We ride the metro all the way east, past stations I've never heard of, and exit onto a street where the houses are even more narrow and clustered together than the triplexes we live in. They have fancy wooden carvings around the roofs and tiny balconies clinging to the stone. Some of them are painted bright colours, like pink or yellow, and they remind me of the gingerbread house in "Hansel and Gretel." I feel I should be dropping a trail of breadcrumbs, to help us find our way back.

"That's the old Edna cookie factory," my grandmother stops and says, pointing up to an abandoned building whose windows are all boarded up.

"They made cookies in there!"

"Yes they did. And we used to play in the yard here. Sometimes the workers would throw down a shower of broken cookies."

"Did you eat them?"

"Of course we did," my grandmother laughs. "We didn't often get treats, not like you kids now." I try to picture a younger version of my grandmother diving at the broken cookies.

At the top of a street called Dorion, Gran stops and takes a deep breath, as though she's bracing herself for what we are about to see.

"This is it," she declares, stretching out her hand and pointing down a street that isn't really a street any more. The cement foundations of some of the houses are still standing, covered in spray paint and graffiti, but the houses themselves have been levelled.

"What happened? Was there some war in Montreal I don't know about?"

My grandmother laughs. "No, sweetie. This is what happened when they built the bridge in 1925. The Jacques Cartier," she says, pointing ahead to the green foot of a bridge that steps onto the street, like the leg of a giant monster.

"They demolished all our houses. Come and I'll show you," my grandmother says mysteriously, as though there are things hidden in the wreckage. We walk to the middle of the street. "This is where I lived," she says, pointing to a square of concrete.

"And this," continues my grandmother, "is where the gypsy lived." She moves her finger over half an inch and smiles. I don't know what to say.

"She lived right beside me, in the last house. She came over from Europe around the time of the Spanish flu, Penny. She had no family at all. And she was so young. She worked as a mother's helper. The family had eight children, and they were a handful, I can tell you! The mother used to tell stories about the odd spices her girl cooked with. And how she decorated her room with colourful scarves. She kept chickens out back, like she used to in her old country, I guess. We would watch her feed and talk to them in her strange language. The mother didn't mind, because her chickens produced perfect eggs. The girl had a magic touch with them, she said.

"Then the family had to move away and they couldn't afford to take her with them — this was later, during the Depression, you know — so she stayed behind. She sold eggs to make money. Back then, she would actually let us kids into the yard to collect our own eggs. She'd wrap them delicately in newspaper, handling them so gently, as if they were alive."

Then my grandmother stops talking and stares straight ahead, as though she's seeing a film in her mind. I want to ask her so many questions, but something tells me to just let her talk and tell the story her own way.

"Anyway, in the end, we all had to leave. My family was moving to Fairmount Street, a few miles west. But it was worse for her. She had no family, no one. She'd come over on her own, on a big ship. It must have been terrible. I'm sure she didn't have a first-class ticket. The police had to evict her. They marched right in and carried out all her stuff, such as it was. She stood right about where we are now, watching." My grandmother sounds really sad, and her expression is a million miles away, as if she's reliving that day so many years ago.

"I only came back twice myself," she continues. "The second time was with my sisters to climb the new bridge — it was called the Harbour Bridge then — right after it opened, to watch the Zeppelin fly overhead. So many people were standing on the bridge, I thought we'd topple over into the river."

I wait for her to tell me what she came back for the first time, but she doesn't. Instead, she says, "We better start heading back. But I wanted you to see it, Penny, since you asked."

"I know, but … You said it was a story about loyalty, about someone you've known for seventy-five years. I still don't know who you're talking about."

"Penny. Can't you guess?"

My mind sifts through pictures of all the people I know. I try to picture a young gypsy girl holding a basket of eggs. Her face is like the girl's in the picture I downloaded this morning, with big brown eyes and a wide smile. Then I age her in my mind, adding white hair and wrinkles. Chicken are clucking around her feet. That's when it hits me. I should have clued in when Gran told me how the girl kept chickens out back. I can't believe the kids back then would actually come into the Queen of Sheba's yard to choose their own eggs. No matter how brave the kids in my neighbourhood might be, they'd never actually go that far. The bravest thing Min, Sharon, Cindy, and I ever did, apart from the bread-and-string trick, was to stand outside and chant, "*Double, double, toil and trouble. Stinky queen come out on the double.*"

Now it occurs to me that the whole time we were doing that, the Queen of Sheba was kind of my grandmother's friend. I stare at their old houses. They were so close together their walls must have touched. I feel a shiver run through me, as though the cold wind that blows off the Saint Lawrence River is chilling my bones.

"How come you never told me? How come I never saw you talk to her?" I ask.

"It's just the way it is, Penny. We were never really friends in the conventional way. We just once knew each other. And she's a terribly private person. Always was, but she got more so with age." After a few minutes, my grandmother says, "We should head back now, Penny. I don't think I can do much more."

Gran does look really tired. It's like her knees are sagging. But she seems tired in a different way, too, as if seeing her old neighbourhood has brought back a lot of memories, both good and bad.

I take a last look down Dorion. I see a long trail of ghost houses, their walls and beams transparent, dipping off into the horizon. At the end of the street I see a wagon, pulled by a horse, heading down toward the river. There's a hub of activity down at the port, where dozens of ships are being loaded. A brass sign over an archway appears, on it the word, *Constanta*. Hundreds of weary-looking people stand around, their clothes tattered. Many of them are children. Their dark eyes look up afraid, right at me. It's one of the pictures I saw this morning, but it fits perfectly into this frame.

"Penny?" My grandmother taps my shoulder.

I follow the green leg of the bridge way up to where it joins with the pillars and curves off into the sky.

Then we head back. When we are walking down our street from the metro, my grandmother turns and flashes a wide smile at the Queen of Sheba's house. I've seen her do this before, and I've always found it so embarrassing. It's not like the Queen is standing there looking out, waiting for someone to smile at her.

"You never know. It doesn't hurt to be friendly," my grandmother always said when I complained.

But today, I don't say a thing.

Chapter 5

"So, what've I missed around here?" Min asks. She's finally recovered from her flu. She and Sharon are over at my place.

"Oh, all kinds of excitement," I say, trying to sound sarcastic. I woke up with images of stone houses, green bridges, and chickens floating around my head. I should tell my friends about the Queen, but I'm not ready yet.

"So did Cindy get Jason yet?" Min asks.

"No, he's still a work in progress," I say. "But she's getting closer."

"Let's call her, see if she wants to join us," says Sharon. "We can help her plan some new strategies." I don't understand why Sharon is so into this Jason scheme. She acts like it would be a victory for all of us if Cindy got a boyfriend. As if she'll be the one walking around on his arm.

Half an hour later the four of us are heading off

to Rockland, a really big mall full of ritzy stores none of us can afford to shop at. We usually look at CDs and electronic stuff, check out the new animals at the pet store, and then have a slice of pizza for two dollars at the food court. Cindy shines at the mall. It's where she can really strut her stuff. Plus she gets to see her reflection over and over in the mirrored walls and shiny glass storefronts.

About a block away from the mall, on l'Acadie, we approach a construction site, where giant shovels are digging out a foundation. They must be putting up another high-rise. The one right beside it is half-done. Cranes are lifting huge steel beams, stacking them like toy bricks in the sky. And beside that one is the completed high-rise, rising way up above us.

"Wow!" says Cindy. "I'd love to move into one of these. They're amazing. Someone told me they have a pool on the top floor. They're so much better than those stubby buildings we live in. I love tall things!"

I watch Sharon's face when Cindy says this. She's trying to be cool, but it isn't working. Her forehead is pinched.

"I'd hate it," Sharon says. "Too many people. And what if the elevators break and you live on the top floor? You'd have to climb a lot of stairs."

"The elevators won't break, stupid. They're new. Everything's new. That's what I like about them," Cindy says forcefully. I have a quick flash of the old streets my grandmother and I walked yesterday, the narrow grey-stone buildings with pointy attic windows. I thought they were beautiful, in a strange way. Telling Cindy about yesterday will be really hard. I wonder if there's a way to tell Sharon and Min, but not Cindy.

We wander around the mall for an hour. I actually find shopping malls pretty boring. It's probably because I've grown up listening to my grandmother. She thinks my generation is obsessed with shopping. I know exactly what wardrobe she had when she was my age: two blouses, two skirts, one pair of shoes, a sweater, and a winter coat and boots. Oh yeah, and all the underwear stuff that they used to wear back then, although she says you couldn't have put her in a corset if you'd paid her.

Cindy's doing her usual routine of trying on really expensive clothes and modelling them in the dressing-room mirrors. She pretends she's going to bring her mother back to make her final decision.

"I'm sure she'll like it, but I have to check with her first. You know, she's the one with the credit card." Cindy flashes a wide smile at the saleslady, who's been complimenting Cindy non-stop since she tried on the red top and black pants. Cindy stands for the longest time in front of the mirror, turning from side to side, as though she can't believe what she sees.

"What do you think, guys?"

We all tell her she looks fantastic. What else is there to say? She does. The black pants make her legs look even longer. And thinner.

"I'll bring her tomorrow, after work," Cindy says, handing the clothes back to the woman. Sure. Cindy's mother spends the day cleaning washrooms in Place Ville Marie, one of Montreal's tallest office buildings. She's usually exhausted when she gets home. That's why Cindy has to do so much. There's no more chance of her running up to Rockland than there is of her being able to afford those expensive clothes.

Finally, we head to the food court.

"Nothing for me today," says Cindy. "I'm still full from breakfast." Min and I roll our eyes. It's two o'clock. Unless she ate breakfast at noon, that can't be true.

The rest of us buy a slice of pizza. Then Cindy just sits there and watches us bite into our slices, piled high with toppings. When her stomach lets out a growl, she hits it, as though it's being bad.

"I'm going to get some water," she says, getting up. She wanders back toward the food counters. About halfway there, a man steps in front of Cindy and starts talking to her. I have no idea who he is. None of us do. We all look at each other and shrug. For a minute I think it might be Cindy's father. Maybe her mother actually sends him Cindy's school picture every year so he knows what she looks like. Maybe, for the first time in fifteen years, he's coincidentally in the same mall at the same time as Cindy.

They seem to be talking for a long time, although he's doing all the talking. Cindy is simply nodding. Then we watch him hand Cindy a piece of paper.

Cindy practically runs back to our table. She's forgotten about her water. "Oh my god, you'll never guess what just happened. That guy, he was a model scout. He said he wants to represent me. He said I have the looks, that I could really make it in the business. Can you believe it? He asked if I've ever thought about modelling. Of course I have. I mean, that's what I want to do."

The rest of us are speechless. I haven't heard Cindy this bubbly since her mother actually let her get a hamster back in grade three.

"That's amazing, Cindy," says Sharon. "What do you have to do?"

"Nothing, just call him. He gave me his card." She lays it out on the table, between our leftover pizza crusts.

The guy's name is Lorne London.

I look over at Min. She is someone who looks at things carefully before deciding what she thinks. She looks very unsure about this.

"Did you tell him you'd do it?" asks Min.

"Of course. Do you think I'm crazy? It's not every day someone offers you a modelling job, you know."

"Good thing you went for water," I say, "otherwise he would've missed you."

"Oh no, he's been watching me. He said he's really selective. He saw me an hour ago. He's just been waiting to get me alone."

The thought that some guy had been stalking us for an hour is creepy, no matter who he is. And why did he have to wait until Cindy separated herself from us? Was it because we're so plain, he couldn't stand the thought of being near us?

Cindy obviously doesn't share any of our concerns. She's holding the card in her palm, pressing it to her chest, then holding it up and rereading it, over and over again.

I think it's the motto along the bottom she likes best: *Taking you to the top*.

It looks to me like Cindy's halfway there.

Chapter 6

The next day at school Cindy is perfectly made up, with blue lids, mascara, and eyeliner, accentuating her hazel eyes. She holds her head high, about a foot above Sharon, who walks beside her.

"Ding, ding," Sharon says suddenly. She and Cindy are walking ahead of me and Min, toward the cafeteria. We see Sharon pointing toward Jason. Then Sharon stops and lets Cindy get ahead, as if she knows it'll ruin Cindy's chances if she's caught with her. We all learned that lesson yesterday, with Lorne London. We watch Cindy walk past Jason, flipping her hair. He smiles at her. She goes up to him and they talk, but we can't hear what they're saying. Whatever it is, it must be funny, because Cindy can't stop laughing. Then the two of them take off in the opposite direction of the cafeteria. I bet she's telling him about being scouted. What guy doesn't want to go out with a model?

We look for Cindy after school, but she's nowhere in sight. She wasn't in any of her afternoon classes either. I wonder if she skipped with Jason.

At the top of our street, we pass the shed that's attached to the back of Ernie's grocery store. We've always called the shed the Rat House. That's because it is supposed to be crawling with rodents at night, although I've never actually seen any. Sometimes, Ernie leaves the back door open and we can see into the butcher section of the store. We watch him haul carcasses onto his work table, where he chops them up.

Today Ernie's out back, taking a cigarette break. He's wearing his bloodstained apron, as usual. He gives us a friendly wave.

"Hello, girls, how are you doing," he says. We wave back, trying not to laugh. I wonder if he knows his shop's nickname.

The moment we walk through my door, I know something is wrong. The house is too quiet. And then I hear muffled voices down the hallway.

"Gran!" I call out. For a second, I have an image of my grandmother and the Queen of Sheba drinking tea together in the kitchen, my grandmother telling her about our trip to their old street on Saturday. How would I explain that to Min and Sharon? Maybe I should find a way to send them home.

But then my mother walks into sight, still wearing her business suit.

"What are you doing here?" I ask. Before she has time to answer, my father appears. Now I know something's definitely wrong. My parents stand side by side, their arms folded across their chests, their heads down. It's the first time I can remember seeing them home in the middle of a work day.

"Where's Gran?" I ask.

"She's been taken ill," my father says.

"She's had an attack," my mother adds.

"What kind of attack?" I snap back at them. Why are they standing there so uselessly, with their arms folded across their chests?

"It was her heart, Penelope. She's at the hospital. They've got her hooked up to all kinds of machines and on I.V. They're doing scans and other tests at this very moment."

"I want to see her."

"You can't. Not today, sweetie. She needs rest. Your mother and I just got back. You'd only be in the way. And she wouldn't even know you were there," my father says.

Wouldn't know I was there? How could that be? My father knows nothing about the hundred secret ways of communicating my gran and I have developed over the years. I'd just have to find her hand, no matter how many tubes were hooked up to it, and squeeze it a certain way, and she'd know it was me.

I shoot my parents a dirty look and march down the hall toward my room. When I pass my grandmother's room I stop and put my hand on the door handle. My mother is right behind me.

"No, no. Don't," my mother calls out, leaping to catch my arm to stop me from opening the door.

I tug hard, freeing myself, and give her a defiant look. Then I step into my grandmother's room. Her bed is empty. The sheets and blankets are bundled up into a little hill, and for a second I think she might be hiding under it, waiting to spring up and surprise me. I run to the bed and start flinging the covers off. But she isn't there. All I find are her pink knit slippers, so worn that the heels are paper thin, curled up where her feet should be.

Chapter 7

The next day I don't bother going to school and nobody comes in to tell me to either. I can hear my parents moving around in the house. They've obviously taken the day off work. The occasional big crash tells me Adam is home too. I guess it was easier than getting him out the door. That's normally my grandmother's job.

At ten o'clock I come out of my room to find my parents sitting at the kitchen table staring into coffee mugs. They're both in their work clothes. It's like they couldn't figure out what else to wear on a Tuesday.

"I want to go see Gran," I announce. My parents look at each other.

"Just wait a while, Penny. It's still early," my father says. "She needs quiet." What does he think I'm going to do — burst in with a trumpet?

"If you don't take me, I'll go myself, by bus. I

know how." And I do, too. Thanks to my grandmother I know the whole intricate web of bus and metro routes leading outwards from this neighbourhood. There isn't a ride out of here to some interesting part of the city that we haven't taken. My grandmother started taking me to Old Montreal when I was little. She loved to visit the Bonsecours Church to see the doll display of the life of Marguerite de Bourgeois. She's also taken me to Île Ste-Hélène, where the Montreal Casino is. She pointed out the pavilions that used to belong to Expo '67, years before I was born.

"Besides, why aren't you guys at the hospital? Don't you want to see how she is?"

My mother looks stung.

"Of course we do! We've already been, early this morning, while you were sleeping. There's no change," my father says. He reaches out to hold my mother's hand.

"I can't believe you went without me. That was so mean. Well, I'm going on my own then. I don't need you to get me there."

"Penny, don't! Wait and we'll all go together in a little while. Please," says my mother.

But I don't listen. I stamp out of the kitchen, get dressed, and run to catch the 80 bus, which takes me down Park Avenue. I get off at Pine, turn right, and walk the short distance to the Royal Victoria Hospital, which is perched at the bottom of the mountain.

I ask what room my grandmother's in at the reception desk. When I get there, she's lying in bed, her head propped up by pillows. An I.V. machine stands like a tall lamp with its electrical cord attached to her arm, its clear liquid lit by the sun shining through the window. More wires spin out from under her flannel nightgown, leading to a machine on a table beside her. Her eyes are open, and she uncurls a finger from the sheet she's clutching with her right hand and motions for me to come closer. My grandmother pats the bed and I sit beside her.

"Are you okay, Gran?" I ask. She nods slowly.

"I had a little attack," she whispers. Her breath smells tinny, like medicine. She pats my hand with her own brown-spotted one.

"Then can you come home?" I ask.

"Well, maybe soon, but not yet. They want to watch me for a while, you know?"

"Was it our trip to your old street, Gran? Did that wear you down?"

"No, silly. It's just my age. I am eighty-five, you know?"

"I know, but you don't act old. I never really think about your age."

"That's because you're young. You don't think about age yet, as well you shouldn't." Then she squeezes my hand. I look down at her hand covering mine, and think about the fact that seventy years separate the two of us. We have so much in common. I can't imagine my grandmother being as close to anyone as she is to me. I bet she wasn't even as close to her husband. She was married at thirty, which was old back then. And that was only because she could no longer resist her parents' pressure to do it. Maybe she was once closer to my mother, when she was younger, before my father became part of the family. And then there are all her friends in the neighbourhood, including, I guess, the Queen of Sheba, in some strange way.

"If you're eighty-five, Gran, how old is the Queen of Sheba?"

My grandmother smiles.

"Let's see, that would make her about ninety or so. No spring chicken!"

I stare at the monitor that my grandmother's attached to, where a green line is drawing waves that remind me of the top of the Jacques Cartier Bridge. Maybe now would be a good time to ask my grandmother to continue the story of the Queen of Sheba. If I'm going to say that this is a family story, I need more to go on.

"Gran, what happened after the eviction?"

"Well, sweetie, she had nowhere to go, so she was moved by the police to the local Salvation Army. I can still see the two policemen who escorted her away, one on either side. They tried to be kind, but they still made her look like a criminal. She was drooped between them, her head hung down so sorrowfully." My grandmother speaks very slowly, her voice barely above a whisper.

"She had to leave everything behind, even her

chickens. The police moved her stuff into her backyard and covered it with a tarp. I guess they didn't know what to do with it all."

One thing I've learned is that gypsies are used to being evicted. Early Christians believed the Roma had made the nails that crucified Christ, so they were rounded up and imprisoned, or driven out of villages all the time, wherever they went.

"People were too busy loading up and moving on themselves, sweetie. Don't forget, we were all evicted. You saw the street."

The concrete foundations of the amputated houses come back to me. I see the street as it must have been before, the brick houses reaching up two or three stories high. Down in the centre of the block, people are gathered, boxes and suit-cases at their feet, awaiting lifts. They're hugging, saying goodbye.

My grandmother has closed her eyes, as though telling this story has exhausted her. I stare off at nothing in particular, a peculiar feeling rising inside me.

Suddenly my parents enter the room. My mother steps toward me. "Penny, you didn't need to take off like that. You could've come with us. We didn't mean that you couldn't ever visit Granny, you know. We just wanted you to wait."

"That's okay, Mom." But I'm glad I came alone. I couldn't have talked to my grandmother about the Queen of Sheba otherwise, not that their con-nection was any clearer now. I bend down and kiss my grandmother's warm forehead. She doesn't budge. Her eyes are closed and she's breathing heavily. I'm afraid I've asked her for too much, that I've drained her. But when I look up at the monitor, I see that the pattern of her heart is still even and steady.

"Sorry, Gran," I whisper into her ear. She squeezes my hand to tell me it's all right.

"I'll see you guys later," I say to my parents.

"Penny, wait and come home with us," my father says.

"No, it's okay. I think I'll walk. I'll see you at home."

"Penny, you can't walk all that way alone, especially not now," says my mother.

But I am determined to do it. I have a lot to think about.

"I'll be okay, Mom, really."

"You're sure?" I nod.

So they just let me go.

Chapter 8

When I get back to school on Wednesday, it's like I've been away for a month — that's how much further Cindy has gotten with Jason. In fact, when I step onto the school grounds, the first thing I see is the two of them, holding hands.

"Told you," says Min. "It's like it happened in one day. First she got a model scout, then she got Jason."

In homeroom we finally get a chance to talk to Cindy ourselves. "So, did you call London yet?" Min asks her. Cindy looks distracted. She keeps looking over our shoulders, into the hallway, probably for Jason.

"Yeah. He's arranging for them to take shots of me."

"Who is they?" Min asks.

"The agency he works for, of course."

"Did they say you could model for them? I

mean, do they have some jobs for you already?" Sharon asks.

"God, you guys. Nothing happens that fast. First I have to get my portfolio together. Lorne said I should do some courses too."

"What kind of courses?" asks Min. "You hate school."

"Courses on important things, like walking and makeup, not the kind of useless stuff we get here," says Cindy.

I don't say a thing. I'm waiting for Cindy to ask me how my grandmother is. I know she must know. Min and Sharon would have told her why I was away yesterday. But she doesn't ask. I guess she has too many other things on her mind.

After class, Jason's waiting for Cindy outside our classroom. She darts over to him and two seconds later they're gone, leaving us in a swirl of whatever perfume she was wearing.

We don't get another chance to talk to her all day. She spends recess and lunch with Jason and his friends. I never imagined Cindy would be part of that gang. They seem so much older than us. And different. As far as I can tell, all they do is stand around posing outside the school. They're all really into the whole clothes-and-looks thing. But, then again, I guess now Cindy is, too.

After school, we stop off in the Old Man Park. It isn't exactly a park. It's more like a big square of grass with two cement paths laid out in an X and lined with benches where old men sit, muttering to each other under old-fashioned hats. We've scraped together enough change for a bag of chips and a chocolate bar, and Sharon volunteers to go buy them at the dépanneur across the street.

"I guess her mission's accomplished," Min says. She doesn't have to tell me who she's talking about.

"Do you mean Jason or the modelling?"

"Both."

"I mean, I guess I'm happy for her. It's what she wanted, right?"

"Yeah, I suppose. But I can't help feeling kind of …"

"Dumped."

"Yeah, I guess so. It's pretty stupid right? I mean, if one of us got a boyfriend, we wouldn't be sitting in the Old Man Park, would we?"

"Hey, Min. Maybe we could find boyfriends in the Old Man Park. Look at that one over there." I point to an old man across from us who's fast asleep. His triple chin is trembling under the collar of his jacket.

"Nah, I prefer that one." Min points to a man who's feeding pigeons. "At least he can stand." We both crack up.

Sharon's almost back at our bench when she drops her bag to the ground and grabs hold of the iron railing of the fence that lines the X. Then she kicks up her feet and spins around, again and again, her hair sweeping the grass as she tumbles.

We clap, but we're also amazed. We used to spend hours spinning after school, but Min and I would whack our heads and get a concussion if we tried that now. Cindy was the best spinner. She'd flip a thousand times, never once feeling woozy. And I was always amazed by the way her hair just bounced back into place without a single tangle. It occurs to me that she'd be perfect in a fast-car commercial, especially one for a convertible. She could get whipped around the countryside by some hunk at a thousand miles per hour, and her hair would just fall back gracefully around her neck, no brush needed.

"Oh my god, I feel sick," Sharon says, holding her stomach. I rip open the bag of chips and we pass it back and forth, then do the same with the chocolate bar. Too bad we didn't have enough money for a drink.

"I have an idea," says Sharon. "Let's finish this stuff with our eyes closed. We'll take turns picking a location and we have to pretend we're there. Okay?" Sharon always has some wacky idea. We're used to it.

"Me first," Sharon continues. "Okay. Right now we're on a beach in California, and it's full of gorgeous guys with ripped bodies. We're sitting on a blanket watching them play volleyball. Some hot guys are surfing in the background. Oh yeah, and we're all really gorgeous too. We're in these skimpy bikinis and we're the only girls on the whole beach."

"Oh my god, Sharon. That would so never happen."

"It's fantasy, Min. Get over it," Sharon responds. "Okay. One, two, three, go." We all close our eyes. I try to picture the beach, borrowing the images from TV shows, the kind where gangs of gorgeous teens spend every waking minute in the sand. But it's so hard to imagine. I put myself in a red bikini and give myself a deep brown tan. My hair's ten shades lighter and ten inches longer. I feel completely stupid. Even when we swim at Jarry Park in the summer, I can't get into the whole tanning thing. I've watched other girls do it, flipping over to even out their colour, like pieces of toast.

"How long do we have to do this?" asks Min. I bet she's having just as much trouble as I am.

"One more minute," says Sharon. I'm sure she's in the middle of the volleyball game, smashing perfect shots over the net. Later, all the guys will pick her up and carry her around, the hero of the game.

"One, two, three, open!" calls Sharon.

The Queen of Sheba is standing in front of us, like she's appeared from nowhere, springing out of the grass. She starts to walk forward, taking tiny measured steps. All three of us suck in our breath at the same time, holding perfectly still. She's staring at us over the top of her eyeglass frames, which have slipped to the tip of her nose, cutting her eyeballs in half. Then, she fixes her eyes on me. I want to get up and run, but I can't move. The Queen takes one step closer, her eyes never blinking, staring at me intently. From the corner of my eyes I see my friends, frozen in awe. Finally, the Queen stops about a foot away, close enough that I could reach out and touch her wrinkled face. After a minute, she opens her mouth and whispers a few words I can't understand, in a foreign language, full of twists and curls. Every now and then an English word pops in, and I hang on to it, but then she starts speaking another language again. My mind races to follow her, but I can't. Her words make me dizzy. Then the word "chickens" hits me loud and clear a couple of times. I think back to Dorion, to what my grandmother told me about the Queen selling eggs. Is she having some kind of flashback, maybe of selling eggs to my grandmother? Could she actually know that something has happened to her? If so, she might know more about me than I thought.

Then the Queen's hand starts stretching toward me, her fingers as pointy as ten newly sharpened pencils. A row of silver bangles tinkles on her wrist. I lean as far back into the bench as I can. Then, just when she's about to touch me, I jump up. My legs are numb, but somehow I manage to make them work. I dodge the Queen's arm and take off. Min and Sharon follow, and we all run until we are safely inside my backyard.

"Oh my god, that was so weird, Penny," says Min, catching her breath.

"Yeah, it's like she wanted to scratch your eyes out," adds Sharon.

"No, it wasn't like that," says Min. "She wasn't angry. It was like … like she knew you or something. Like she recognized you."

I see the Queen bending toward me, peering intently into my eyes.

I remember reading that Roma women who tell fortunes are called *drabardi*. I wonder if the Queen is one of them.

Chapter 9

On Friday, my grandmother is moved to a nursing home to recover. I think she can recover better at home, in her own room, but my parents disagree.

"She needs constant care, someone to look after her," my mother tries to explain to me.

"I can look after her," I say. "I can bring her whatever she needs before and after school. We'd just need someone to look in a couple of times during the day. I could even come home at lunch."

"It won't work, Penny," my father says. "She needs more than that. Do you know how to get an old woman in and out of the bath on your own? They have special equipment for all these things at the home. She'll be well cared for there."

What they really mean is that neither of them can be bothered. It would interfere too much with their jobs. Sometimes they act like they're somewhere on Wall Street, instead of just loans officers in a small Canadian bank. Like the stock market would come crashing down without them.

My mother and I visit my grandmother on Saturday. The nursing home is a huge grey-stone building all the way out east, at the very end of Saint-Catherine Street. My mother has to drive us along Notre Dame Street to get there. The Saint Lawrence River runs alongside us, to our right. On the other side of it, I can see the Ferris wheel and twisty tracks of roller coasters over at La Ronde, which is closed now for the season. When we pass under the Jacques Cartier Bridge, I crane my neck left as far as it will go to find the foot of the bridge stepping down around Dorion, but I can't see it from here. I hope my grandmother can see the bridge from her bedroom window. It might make her feel that she's come full circle, that she's sort of back home again, where she started.

But when I step into her room, I see how foolish I've been. Hers is one of six beds, and she's nowhere near the window. Even if she were, all she'd see is a brick wall with a fire escape zigzagging down from the building across the alley.

"Hi, Mom," my mother says.

"Hi, Gran," I add. My grandmother just kind of grunts in our direction. She tries her best to smile, but it's forced, I can tell. I'm amazed by how thin she looks. A nurse and an orderly are helping her into a wheelchair. They lift her up under her armpits and lower her into the seat, then tuck rolled-up towels beside her. They put extra towels on her left side. Finally, the nurse lays my grandmother's left arm across her lap. I notice for the first time just how floppy the whole left side of her body seems to be.

"Are you okay, Gran?" I ask her. She looks so uncomfortable and cramped between the bars of her chair.

"I'm okay. I just don't really like being here too much, my precious." I'm glad she still remembers to call me that. I haven't heard it in a while.

"Is the food good?" my mother asks like she knows it won't be.

"It's all right, but I'm not used to eating around so many people. And most of them don't eat. They kind of let the food dribble down their chins until one of the nurses scoops it back in." I make a face. That would make me lose my appetite, too.

"And you see that one over there?" my grandmother asks, pointing to a bald, frail woman who seems to be sleeping. "She howls all night long, like she's just lost a child. It's so creepy, I can't sleep."

I glance at my mother. She looks like she's about to cry.

"I'm sorry, Mom. But the doctor said you needed watching," she says in a soft and strained voice.

Then we're all silent. There doesn't seem to be much to say. We wheel my grandmother down the hall to the lounge and place her beside a coffee table. My mother and I sit at a small sofa facing her. The room has a large picture window that looks out on a small terrace. Some geraniums are still clinging to window boxes outside, in spite of early October winds. The room is also full of potted plants, some of which reach as high as the ceiling. My mother unwraps the egg-salad sandwiches I helped her make earlier. She spreads out a napkin on my grandmother's lap and places a couple of sandwiches on it. My grandmother lifts a square with her right hand and takes little bites. It's pretty clear she isn't really enjoying the meal at all. She usually loves to eat, probably because food was scarce when she was young. She always says that it's such a pity to watch so many young girls today fight with food, like it's their enemy.

Watching her eat is painful, so I look instead at the patients who surround us in the lounge. The old women have white hair like my grandmother, and are sitting in wheelchairs like her, but they seem to be in really bad shape, slouched way forward, as though their bones can't hold them up. Their guests have to feed them, like babies. Many are muttering to themselves or laughing at nothing in particular. I can't see my grandmother as one of these old people. Up until last week she was up and about, baking, complaining about the stupidity of politicians, walking around the city. In a million years she could never look like these old women. It's just an accident that she's here. Someone will eventually see their mistake and send her home.

Then I look up to see my mother shovel a blob of escaped egg salad back into my grandmother's mouth. All of her concentration seems centred on chewing up the bits. When she finally swallows, she looks at me and shrugs, as though excusing herself.

I want to ask her so many things, to really talk like we used to, to hear her tell one of her stories about long ago, but she looks so tired, and she's so quiet, that I can't think of a way of starting. So we all just sit and stare out at the bright red geraniums, occasionally taking sips of our drinks and trying to smile.

"I'm going to go speak to the nurses before we go," my mother eventually says. "You and Penny can have a chat."

"So, Gran. Do you think you'll be home soon?" I ask, trying to sound perky. She just shrugs, like she doesn't want to talk about it.

I wanted to ask her more questions about the Queen of Sheba, especially after what happened at the Old Man Park. I still don't know how the Queen ended up on the same street as my grandmother again, like when they were young. But the last time I quizzed her, at the hospital, it really wore her out. Besides, I can already see my mother walking down the hallway toward us. I guess the nurses didn't have much to say.

"We'd better go now, Mom," my mother announces, as though she can't stand to be there anymore. "Do you want us to wheel you back to your room?"

"It's okay love. I'll stay here." I'm glad when

she says this. I'd rather think of her in this sunny plant-filled room than back in her dingy bedroom, across from the howling woman.

"Goodbye, Gran." I bend down to kiss her. The white hair on her head is so thin, I can see the brown spots of her scalp underneath.

I wait for her to say, 'Bye, my precious' but she doesn't. She lifts her hand and waves at us instead. I wonder if she'll keep waving, even after we've left the building, like some sort of wind-up doll.

"Why does she need to sit in a wheelchair?" I ask my mother as we head toward the parking lot.

"Because it wasn't just a small heart attack like she says. She's had a stroke, Penny. Your grandmother may never walk again. She can't move her left side at all. You don't think I want to leave her there, do you?" My mother stops walking and glares at me.

A stroke! Nobody told me that. I guess that explains her floppiness.

"I guess not," I reply, uncertainly.

"Well, let's get one thing straight, Penelope. Of course I don't. Many old people are put into homes like this and worse, even before they get sick. I have always kept her with me. Have you ever thought of that? She's lived with us for seventeen years, since before you were born. And she's the reason we never moved away. Don't you think your father and I would like to move somewhere else, to buy a house maybe, in a nicer part of the city, somewhere we could have our own yard, where we don't have other people living on top of us. It's because of her that we stayed, so that she could stay in familiar territory, near all the neighbours she's known for so long."

"Sorry," I say. I know I can't explain any of this to her, so I don't bother trying. I follow her quietly into our car and stare out the window the whole time she's driving us home. The half-hour passes in a flash, and before I know it, we're turning onto our street. As we drive past the Queen's house, I examine it intently, wondering what she's doing inside. She must lead such a lonely life, imprisoned behind her heavy curtains and thick bushes.

I wonder if she can sense that my grandmother is no longer living on this street. And, by the looks of it, probably never will again.

Chapter 10

Cindy's hanging out with Jason all the time now. It's like she's off in another world, one the rest of us don't belong to. The same thing happened two years ago, when Cindy first got her period. She stopped hanging out with us for a while because none of us had started menstruating yet. She said we couldn't understand what it was like.

That time though, she came back to us a week later, when the bleeding had stopped.

I try catching her eye in class, but she's staring into space, or down at her books, lost in thought. Dreaming of Jason, I guess. Other times, she looks like she can't hold her head up, she's so tired. She keeps yawning. Then her head will collapse onto her thin arms and she'll actually catnap in class. It's not normal to be this tired. Maybe it's those modelling classes she mentioned. Maybe they're more demanding than they sounded. I keep waiting for one of the teachers to yell at her, but no one seems to notice.

No one except me. And I wish I didn't. I keep telling myself to just cancel Cindy out of my mind like she's cancelled me. But that's not so easy to do when you've been friends with someone for seven years. We used to talk for hours, about all kinds of things. She slept over at my place a lot when we were little, on nights when her mother would go out. Sometimes, Cindy and I would try to stay up to watch her mother come home. Once, we caught her coming out of a taxi with some guy Cindy had never seen before. Her mother was wobbling up the front stairs on high heels and the guy was steadying her from behind, with his hands on her hips. Cindy didn't want to talk about it and she never mentioned it again, not once, and I knew better than to ask.

Sharon seems lost without Cindy. She's trying a new hairstyle, one with short spiky pieces sticking up on the top. She's hoping it'll make her look taller, but I think it makes her look like a rooster. Every time Cindy and Jason walk by, Sharon looks at them wistfully.

"I can't stand the way they walk right past us," she says one day. "It's like, so insulting." It's the first time I've ever heard Sharon criticize Cindy.

"It doesn't bother me," says Min. "At least we can do what we want now. We don't have to watch out for Jason."

"Yeah, no more bloody ding-donging," Sharon

says angrily. She used to ding with such gusto. It must be worse for her than for us. She was so desperate to have a special role in Cindy's life.

We're standing in the lobby near the front door. No one's going out at lunch today because we're having one of those freak early snowstorms, our first of the year. The wind is swirling the snow around in circles and we can barely see the street from here. The lobby is crowded, full of little huddles, like ours. Way in the back corner, near the hall to the gym, I catch sight of Cindy.

"There she is," I say, nodding with my chin. Cindy's arms are wrapped around Jason's waist, and his arm is draped over her shoulder. But he's talking to some guy over her head. Just at that moment, Cindy looks up and her eyes dart straight across the lobby to mine. We hold each other's stare. She's looking at me blankly, like I'm a complete stranger, one she's decided not to like. It's the look she used to have in her eyes when she was little and her mother would leave her in the schoolyard early. Cindy would stand up in the front of the line glaring at the other kids, who arrived holding their parents' hands, kissing and hugging goodbye. It's the look that said "You all think you're better than me, but I don't care because I'll show you one day."

I guess she thinks she's showing us now. But, I can't help thinking that she should look happier.

Then Jason swings Cindy around and they take off toward the back exit. There's an overhang there that kids smoke under. Last year, the school introduced this new policy allowing kids to smoke in that one spot. Parents didn't like it, but the principal said they did it to stop kids from going down the lane to smoke near the elementary school, which set a bad example for the young kids. I wonder if Cindy's smoking now too. I remember her telling me smoking kills your appetite, as if that was a good thing.

"Do you guys want to come over?" It's the first time I've invited anyone in since my grandmother went away. It's just not the same coming home without her. The house is quiet, except for Adam doing his boy thing, and there hasn't been any home baking.

But today is different. I smell it right away, the mix of brown sugar and chocolate. For a second, I think Gran might have recovered, that she's actually back home. I'll find her in the kitchen, pulling something out of the oven with her old, worn oven mitts.

But it's not her, it's my father. He's standing over a tray of slightly burned chocolate-chip cookies. And he's wearing my grandmother's apron over his grey suit. My friends chuckle behind me.

"Penny," he says when he sees me. He sounds surprised, as if he'd forgotten about me. It's only then that I notice my mother sitting at the table behind him, her head in her hands, her back heaving up and down.

"What's the matter?" I ask. "What's going on?"

"Your friends should go home I think, honey. Come and sit down." My father pulls out the chair beside my mother. I sit down and watch my friends turn back toward the door.

"It's Granny. She died just a few hours ago," he says.

My body turns hard. I feel like the piece of celery my science teacher dipped into dried ice today. It turned so stiff he could hammer a nail into a board with it.

My mother's still crying. She doesn't even look at me.

"Penny, are you all right?" I hear my father ask. He pulls my head toward his chest. I can feel his fingers stroking my hair. I don't think my father's ever done that before. It feels nice, but strange.

We stay like that for a long time, until Adam comes racing into the kitchen, saying he can't find his helmet. He wants to cycle in the snow. When he sees us, he stops dead.

"What's up?" he calls out. I wonder if he, too, was fooled by the smell of my father's baking.

"Sit down, Adam," I hear my father say. It's Adam's turn now, but I don't want to hear that horrible word again. So, I get up and float toward my room.

My body stays numb for the rest of the day.

Chapter 11

When I wake up, the fact of my grandmother's death is wrapped tightly around me, like the white cloth of a mummy. All day, every time I breath, I take it in again. I think about our visit to the nursing home on Saturday, just five days ago. I remember the way my grandmother looked, sitting in her chair, waving goodbye slowly, sadly. We should have gone again on Sunday. I don't know why we didn't. I overheard my mother telling my father that the visit had been hard, that she'd almost broken down when she saw my grandmother with all those other sick old people.

I felt the same way, but still, we should have forced ourselves to go back. Maybe Gran had sat there waiting for us to show up, her eyes glued to the clock on her night table, or to the big round clock in the lounge, watching the hours crawl by, wondering when we'd come.

Maybe her last thoughts about us were as people who had disappointed her. We'd abandoned her because she was sick and hard to look at.

She'd have been especially disappointed with me, Penelope. My grandmother chose my name. She said she liked the story of Penelope, who'd waited faithfully for twenty years for Ulysses to come back from his travels.

Only my grandmother was the Penelope in this case, and it was me who didn't come back.

Down the hall, I hear my friends asking for me at the door, and my father mumbling some response. I look at my clock radio and am amazed to discover that it's already four o'clock. School's over. Two seconds later, my father's knocking at my door.

"Penny, your friends want to come in and see you. Is that okay?"

I'd rather pull the blankets way up over my head and hide, but next thing I know, Min and Sharon are in my room.

"Hi, Penny. Are you okay? I'm sorry about your grandmother," Min begins. Her eyes look watery, like she may have been crying.

"Yeah, me too," adds Sharon. We're all quiet for a while. I feel like each of us is remembering my grandmother in some way. For my friends, it's got to be as the old woman with longish white hair who baked delicious treats and told stories about what life was like for girls long ago. She once told us how she'd had to fight with her parents to be allowed to go to Ottawa with her girlfriend on their own, unchaperoned, when they were eighteen. As the train pulled out of the station, she'd never felt so free in her life, knowing she wouldn't be watched for two whole days.

It was the type of story that made us all appreciate who we were.

"How do you feel?" asks Min finally.

"It's just so sudden," I say. "I don't know how I feel."

I look up and see a tear running down Sharon's cheek. It's like she tried to stop it, but it escaped anyway. I haven't even cried yet, and she was *my* grandmother. I wondered if that's normal? Maybe I didn't love her as much as I thought I did.

"Why don't you get dressed and come hang out with us. You can't just stay in your bed all day," says Min.

"Okay. Give me a few minutes."

I join them out back and we sit on the steps, our faces tipped toward the autumn sunshine. It doesn't seem right that it should be such a beautiful day. Torrents of rain should be bursting out of dark clouds, like they would be in some dramatic book or movie. But the air is as dry as I am.

"When's the funeral?" asks Min.

"I don't know. I don't know anything. I haven't even talked to my Mom today. She's been in my grandmother's room all day with the door closed."

I wish Min hadn't mentioned the funeral. I've never been to a funeral. I've only seen them on TV.

"I've never seen a dead body before," I confess.

"Well, maybe you won't have to look at her," says Min.

"Of course I will. The family always does."

"I saw my aunt in her coffin when I was five, and the undertaker had put so much makeup on her I barely recognized her," says Sharon.

The thought of my grandmother all made up is scary, and wrong. She never even wore makeup when she was alive. She said it made her feel like a clown.

"My mom wanted me to kiss her cheek, too. She even pulled a chair up beside the coffin for me, but I started kicking and screaming. There was no way I was going to do that. It was too gross."

I want to explain to Sharon that it's not the grossness of seeing someone dead that bothers me. It's the fact that it's my grandmother. I think I'd want to try to shake her awake.

"Will you guys come?" I ask. "I mean, if you want to."

"Of course," they both say together.

"Your grandmother was cool," says Min. "Remember when she used to play that old Elvis record and sing along? My grandmother'd never do that." Min's grandmother looks like one of those apple dolls, with wrinkled sunken cheeks. Min said she had a hard life in the country in China, and it shows.

"Yeah, your grandmother always made me feel … well, you know, normal," says Sharon, her voice cracking.

It was a mistake coming outside. I'm really not ready for this conversation. "I better go back in now," I say. "I'll see you guys later."

My mother's in the kitchen, filling the sink with hot, soapy water. Our good dishes, the ones she normally uses only at Christmas, are stacked on the counter beside her.

"What are you doing, Mom?" I ask. It seems to me she should be too upset to be doing housework.

"I have to get stuff ready for the funeral Saturday," she responds. Her eyes are red and puffy. I guess she's been crying, which is more than I've done.

"Oh, is it that soon?"

"Yeah, two o'clock, at Houseman's, in case any of your friends want to come." I wonder if she was listening at the back door. "Tomorrow you can help me do up some sandwiches. There will be a lot of people at the reception, you know. Your grandmother knew lots of people." My mother seems to be talking about her so casually, but she keeps sniffling in between her words.

I slip away and wander quietly down the hall to my grandmother's old room. What was my mother doing in here before? I hesitate before opening the door, fearful of what I might find. For a frightening second. I imagine my grandmother herself is stretched out on her old bed. But that's nonsense. She's at the funeral home, being cleaned up, like the dishes.

I turn the knob, push the door, and step into the room with my eyes closed, like I used to do when I was little, pretending I couldn't see. I don't need sight. This room is as familiar to me as my own. I might even have crawled around in here, trailing my security blanket, long before I could walk. I stretch out my arms, ready to feel my way around. I haven't taken two steps before I stumble on something hard.

"What the …" I begin to shriek, opening my eyes. At my feet is a cardboard box, so full its sides bulge. The top is taped down, and on the side the words, "Mom's things," are scribbled in black marker.

On her bed sit three more boxes, and on her bureau another two. They all say the same thing. Her belongings sure don't amount to very much — five boxes for a whole lifetime.

The room is completely bare. The bed has been stripped down to the striped mattress, the walls freed of the pictures my grandmother had hung there. It reminds me of her hospital room, only emptier.

I fling open her cupboard door. It's empty, too. There's no trace of my grandmother left. She has been packaged away, ready to be shipped. Then I remember my mother's confession, about how we stayed on this street for so long because of my grandmother. Maybe this is a sign that we'll be leaving. Soon the whole house could be boxed up like this.

Next thing I know I'm tearing open the boxes. Most of them are full of clothes, nothing I'd want to keep, but in a box on her bureau, I find the old toffee tin where she kept odds and ends. I spread out its contents in front of me on my Gran's bed. I've seen some of this stuff before. It's an odd collection of memorabilia: old ticket receipts from plays seen long ago in theatres that have probably been torn down, pictures of herself as a young woman. I love the one of her and a friend sitting on the running board of an old-fashioned car. They look young and happy, laughing up at the camera. I pick up a slip of paper that's flaking off around the edges. It's the old streetcar ticket. On it the words, "Station Jean Talon Station — Five Cents," are still visible. At the bottom of the tin, under more papers, are some tiny bits of broken eggshell. I pick up a few. They are painted different colours, some of them with a bit of pattern or design, part of a leaf, snowflake or diamond. I wonder if they once all fit together, but got smashed somehow.

I wonder if my mother smashed it when she was boxing up all this stuff up? She probably just threw it all together without thinking. It's like she's evicting my grandmother and her memory, boxing her off to some Salvation Army. As if she can't bear any piece of her to remain in our house.

The last thing that catches my eye is a piece of yellowed paper I've never seen before. I unfold it carefully, so it doesn't disintegrate, and uncover a string of words written with a very shaky hand in black ink: *"Thanks you for rescu chickens. You are very brave girl. Your friend, Karika."*

There's only one person I know who has chickens — the Queen of Sheba. I see her old yard, barely big enough to hold the coop. Is the note about those chickens, all the way back on Dorion, seventy-five years ago? The chickens would have been evicted along with everyone else. Does this mean my grandmother saved them? If so, I wonder how she did it, and why she didn't tell me? After all, that was why she took me to Dorion, to give me the family story I was looking for. Why stop halfway?

I fold the note gently and put it back into the tin, along with the rest of the memorabilia. I want to run into the kitchen and shake it in my mother's face, but she might make me give it back if I do, so I hide it instead under my T-shirt, and sneak it across the hall to my room. I can hear my mother calling me. I hope she hasn't heard me rifling around in my grandmother's room.

"What?" I call back.

"I need you to go to Ernie's for me." My mother hands me a list of items: olives and crackers and cheese spread, party stuff.

"What's all this for?" I ask. My mother's acting

like she's preparing for a birthday party, not a funeral.

"For the funeral. Please don't ask questions, just go." She shoos me away with her hands, then turns back to the sink, where she's still washing our good dishes.

With the list tucked in my back pocket I head off up the street. As I pass the Queen's house, an eerie feeling that I'm being watched hovers over me.

At the grocery store I hand my mother's list to Mrs. Ernie. There's no way I want to try to find those things myself. She sighs, like she usually does, as she reads it. Mr. Ernie is at the meat counter in the back, wearing his usual blood-stained overalls.

When Mrs. Ernie returns, I impulsively ask her for one more thing.

"May I please borrow a pen?" I use my politest voice, so she can't say no.

She pulls one out from under the cash register. It's greasy and dusty, but it will do. I turn over my mother's shopping list and, while Mrs. Ernie is packing the bags, I scribble a note to the Queen of Sheba. Or I guess I should start thinking of her as Karika.

Dear Karika, My grandmother, Elaine O'Grady, has died. Her funeral will happen Saturday at the Houseman Funeral Home on Park Avenue at two o'clock. She will probably be buried near her husband at the Mount Royal Cemetery. Regards, Penelope, her granddaughter.

I barely know what I'm doing, but something inside tells me my grandmother would want her to know. She did, somehow or other, rescue the Queen's closest allies — her chickens. The Queen of Sheba has a right to know her friend's final home.

"Thanks," I say, handing back the pen and picking up the bags of stuff.

The bleached picket fence has always stood like a moat between the Queen's house and our street. I can't believe I'm about to cross it. Her rickety front porch may never have held any footsteps other than her own. Her ears will recognize the footsteps of a stranger. But I can't let that stop me.

I creak open the gate and leave my bags beside it, to make myself lighter. Then, as softly as my feet will carry me, I climb the steps. As my heart beats and sweat breaks out on my forehead, I tell myself she might just assume I'm the postman. The hinge on the letter slot squeaks loudly, like a deep scream in a horror film. It seems to go on forever, even after I've dropped in the note. Then I turn and run back down, forgetting about being quiet. I grab my bags, then swing the gate closed behind me.

The Queen's front curtains glide shut, and the shadow of a body steps back from its spot against the dusty glass.

Chapter 12

Friday evening we have to go to the funeral home for what is called "the visitation." I let out a huge sigh of relief when I discover my grandmother's coffin is closed. I don't know why I expected it to be open, except that in movies the coffin always is. I guess it makes the story more dramatic.

"Are you okay, Penny?" my mother asks, taking my hand and squeezing it.

"I thought I'd have to look at her," I confess. The weight slips from my shoulders.

"Oh, honey. Why didn't you tell me you were so worried about that? I could've told you." I don't know why I didn't. It's habit, that's all. I've always turned to my grandmother for help, not my mother.

My parents and I have to stand around all evening welcoming people who've come to pay their respects. There are lots of old women from the neighbourhood, and some who've moved on to other places. I've met all of them at one time or another. They seem to have lots of affection for my grandmother. They tell me how much I've grown, and a couple of them go on and on about how much I look like her. On a side table there's a large black-and-white picture in a gold frame of my grandmother in her early twenties. She's resting her chin on folded hands, her head tilted to the side. There's a playful smile on her face, as though she's thinking about something funny.

"It's all around the eyes, dear," one of the old women says.

"And the mouth. Don't forget the mouth," another joins in.

Even Ernie and his wife show up. It's the first time I've ever seen Ernie without his apron on. My mother seems touched by their visit. She shakes hands with Ernie for a long time. Mrs. Ernie still has folded arms. I wonder if they ever unfold, or if she's held them like that for so long the bones have fused, like a permanent pretzel.

"Your grandmother was a very kind woman," Ernie says to me. I smile, but it seems like an odd thing to say. She only knew Ernie and his wife as people who ran the corner store, I think.

The evening kind of whips by, and before I know it, it's Saturday and I'm sitting in between my parents on a church pew. The coffin is up at the front, horizontal on the stage, to the right of the minister. Many of the same people who visited the funeral home last night are here, along with many more who weren't.

While the service is going on, I try very hard not to think of my grandmother's body lying just beyond the thin layer of reddish wood. I concentrate instead on the coffin itself, telling myself that it's just wood. A harmless wooden box. There is no body inside. It means nothing.

The minister says a prayer about a shepherd, who, my grandmother is supposedly walking with through a green pasture. I try to picture her in the country, surrounded by sheep, but I can't. She spent her whole life in the city. The only animals she knew were sparrows, squirrels, cats, and dogs. And the Queen's chickens, of course.

When the minister talks about the Lord anointing my grandmother's head with oil, I remember how, when I was little, she used to rub menthol ointment into my temples and onto my chest when I had a cold.

When the minister announces that she will live in the house of the Lord forever, I tell myself she's already there, wherever there might be. She is definitely not here in the same room as us, inside that coffin.

I glance across the aisle and spot Min and her parents on the other side of the church. Min sends me a little wave and smiles. Beside them sit Sharon and her mother. Sharon is staring straight ahead, her eyes fixed on the back of Cindy's head. Cindy's with her mother, too. I'm surprised to see them, but I'm glad they came. My grandmother did a lot for Cindy's mother when we were kids.

My father and three men in black surround my grandmother's coffin, lift it, and carry it down the long centre aisle. When it passes us, my mother takes my hand and squeezes. As we follow the coffin out of the church, she is squeezing so hard I feel my bones squish together. Adam is walking beside me, and for once he's acting normal. I was afraid he'd take off screaming after having to sit still for a whole hour. I place my free hand on his shoulder, just in case.

My father helps the men slide the coffin into the back of the hearse, then joins my mother in the front of our car. My hand still feels my mother's grip. Adam and I sit in the back. He's so calm, I wonder if someone drugged him behind my back. When my father pulls out to follow the hearse, Adam does something he's never done before. He puts his head in my lap. It feels funny at first, but soon I'm running my fingers through his thick, brown hair.

Before long we are rolling through the black iron gates of the Mount Royal cemetery. I realize I haven't given much thought to the actual burial. I was too busy worrying about open coffins. But now I know I couldn't stand to see my grandmother being lowered into a hole in the ground. She hated small, dark places.

"Mom, could I stay here?" I ask when we've parked. "I really want to stay in the car."

"Will you be all right alone?"

"I can watch Adam. He's really conked out."

My mother looks at my father and he nods, as if to say he doesn't see any problem. As I watch my parents walk off, hand in hand, every muscle in my body lets go. I hadn't realized I was so tense. The men from the funeral home carry the coffin, the long line of mourners following behind, until they stop and gather in a semicircle not too far from the car. Suddenly my eyes are drawn to a dark figure standing in a group of white birch trees that lies between our car and the plot. It could be another tree, a darker variety imported from some faraway land, it stands so tall and still.

When my grandmother is finally buried, everyone turns to head back. Most people walk solemnly, their heads bowed slightly. I look to the trees, but too late. The tall figure has already left its post. I can see it weaving in and out slowly, avoiding the gravel path that everyone else is on, heading in the direction of the car Adam and I are sitting in. I slouch down in my seat, hoping I can't be seen. But when the figure is directly in front of me, it stops. Two eyes stare at the back window, behind which I'm cowering. Then the Queen's face grows younger, her skin tighter, her hair redder. She nods and bows her head. I watch in awe as her thin lips mouth the words "Thank you."

Then she turns and leaves the cemetery through the magnificent iron gates.

When she's gone, I do what I haven't been able to do since my grandmother died. I cry. My tears are warm, salty, and comforting. It's as though the Queen of Sheba's words have knocked down a wall of numbness that was inside me from the minute my father told me the news of my grandmother's death.

Who would've thought the Queen of Sheba would help tear it down?

Chapter 13

On Monday we all return to our routines: My parents go off to the bank, Adam I walk as far as we can together, then he turns left toward the elementary school and I keep going straight toward my high school. I feel really disconnected from school, even though I hadn't missed that many days. It seems like ages ago that Sharon, Min, and I were hanging out with Cindy, ding-donging whenever we saw Jason.

I kind of sleepwalk through my classes all day. It's like what the teachers are saying suddenly doesn't seem important. I even have a few quizzes I didn't know about. The teachers say not to worry. Just to do my best. I hear my grandmother telling me how much she wanted to continue her education, back when most girls didn't go past elementary school. I wonder how different her life would have been if she could have continued.

Maybe she would have become someone really big and important.

Except she already was really big and important — to me. I also wonder what she'd say to me, watching me let my good grades slip away.

I don't have to wonder for long, though. She'd say I was wasting my intelligence. So, I try to revive myself a bit, and by Wednesday, I'm taking notes in class and trying to focus on what the teachers are saying. But it all seems like really hard work.

That afternoon, when we hit the top of our street, we notice a big crowd standing on the sidewalk near the Queen of Sheba's house. For a terrible second, I think maybe the adults are joining the kids in one of their pranks. Maybe they're all throwing stones together, or tricking the Queen into coming out so they can laugh at her. But when we get close enough, I can see there's an ambulance parked by the curb, its back doors wide open We reach the house just in time to see two ambulance technicians wheel out the Queen of Sheba.

It seems like the whole street is gathered outside to watch. Adam and his friends are weaving in and out of people's legs to get a better view. The Queen's body, up to her neck, is tucked under a white sheet on the stretcher. Her long red-grey hair flows over it. She seems smaller than usual. Her eyes are shut, and the expression on her face is hard and sore. I wonder if she's aware of all the people watching her, and is just faking the need to close her eyes so she doesn't have to look at anyone. I'm sure all the gawking eyes are as painful to her as whatever is wrong with her body.

I'm probably the only person standing here who is even aware of her real name. I say it in my head — *Karika*. It sounds like the name of a queen. She could be one right now, being carried around by her royal subjects.

Beside me, Sharon is pinching her nose and crying, "Pee-yew," as though the Queen has left a trail of bad odour. I want to scream at her. The Queen of Sheba doesn't smell, I'm sure of that. Belittling her is just a game, one we all played for too long. Nothing has changed since the Middle Ages, when her ancestors were blamed for all sorts of things.

I want to turn to tell Sharon how the Queen of Sheba actually came to pay her last respects to my grandmother at the cemetery. But I'm too angry. Besides, she'd probably just find that gross, too.

And then she'd want to know why.

Cindy and Jason are also here, their arms hooked together. Cindy looks tired. She has dark circles under eyes, and her skin is really pale. Usually she'd try to hide that sort of imperfection under loads of makeup. I wonder if she's told Jason just how much our days revolved around pestering the Queen of Sheba in the past, how even she teased the Queen and her chickens enthusiastically not so long ago. But she probably hasn't. It would make her sound too babyish.

Cindy's eyes follow the stretcher as it passes near her. I watch her face for some kind of reaction, but there isn't any. Cindy used to shudder whenever she got a glimpse of the Queen of Sheba, she found her so ugly. But now, there's nothing. She doesn't even wince.

Jason pulls her arm, letting her know he wants to leave. Cindy's about to turn, but then she looks over at us and shrugs. I can't tell if the shrug is related to Jason pulling her away against her will, or if it's related to the Queen and the fact that we can't do anything about her.

Somehow I think that, for the briefest second, Cindy wishes she could be standing with us instead of Jason, as part of the former Queen of Sheba hit squad. It just seems like we belong together today.

Eventually, Jason and Cindy move on, along with the rest of the crowd. The Queen never mattered much, and now she'll be forgotten, along with her beautiful name.

That night, my mother tells us that Mrs. Ernie had said that the Queen was discovered by the postman, who reported something suspicious to the police. He claimed she always pulled the curtain back when he came, without fail, and that he hadn't seen it move for two days.

"Lucky for her she still gets mail," my father says.

"Yeah, but that's not all," my mother continues. "Mrs. Ernie heard she was found on her floor in the kitchen, curled up on the linoleum, and that her chickens were trying to peck her body."

I can't believe my mother is acting like any of this might be true.

"That's ridiculous," I say. "People have nothing better to do than spread stupid gossip. The Queen loved her chickens. She treated them well. They'd never do that to her."

"Take it easy, Penny. I'm just telling you what I heard."

The thought of the Queen's chickens reminds me of that note I found in my grandmother's tin, the one thanking her for rescuing the Queen's chickens. What will happen to the chickens now? I bet nobody has thought about them at all. They're probably clucking around in her backyard, looking for food. I wait until everyone's finished eating and my parents are washing the dishes. While their backs are turned, I grab a loaf of old bread from the breadbox and leave by the back door. If they notice, they don't say anything.

I step cautiously into the Queen's backyard. It's so odd to be inside a place that I've stalked from the outside for so long. But I don't feel scared at all. After all, the Queen can't come out. And even if she did, why would I be scared? I know her name now — Karika. I could pretend I was one of the young kids on Dorion she sold eggs to, back when she still let kids into the yard. Back when she had no reason to distrust them, before the teasing began.

As far I can see, there are only four chickens. Somehow, whenever I pictured her birds in my mind, she had dozens. And up close they look raggedy. They're not the fierce-jowled semi-werewolves we used to exaggerate them to be when we were younger.

I crouch down, rubbing my fingers together and clucking. I have no idea how to call a chicken, and I don't know what I'd do with them if I did manage to catch them. I can't take them home. My parents won't even let me have a cat.

I just about have one when it squawks and flaps away, backing further into the deep grass. If only I had something to loop around their necks, but that might not work. I want to catch them, not kill them.

After an hour, I give up. They're too scared of me, and no wonder. The woman who fed, loved, and cared for them is gone. It's funny, I think, I kind of understand how the chickens feel.

I decide to just leave them some food, so I break up the bread and throw pieces into the high grass near the coop.

But when the bag is empty, I realize I can't just leave them here. It doesn't seem right. I don't know what to do, though. They won't let me near them. Then I have a crazy idea: Ernie. His shop is just a stone's throw away, up the street. Of course, it's perfect — abandoned birds, a butcher. Not that I want Ernie to kill them, but at least he has experience with chickens in some shape or form. He might be willing to help me.

I walk up the lane and knock on the back door of Ernie's store. He'll only be able to hear me if he's in the butcher shop. A minute later he comes out, wearing his butcher's apron, which is spotted in the pale brownish-red colour of blood.

"The Queen's chickens," I say, in one quick breath.

"What?" answers Ernie. "The chickens! What about them?"

"Well, we can't just leave them there. They'll die. They have no one to feed them," I say.

"I see, of course," he says, rubbing his chin with his stained fingers. "You leave them to me. I'll take care of them."

"What do you mean, you'll take care of them?" I say, my eyes straying to the cleaver in Ernie's hand.

"I wouldn't hurt them, my dear. The Queen was a fantastic woman. Terribly misunderstood."

"I want to help you," I say. "I *need* to help you."

"Sure, sure. Here, you take this box." Ernie hands me a wooden box made of slats with plenty of air holes. Then we head back down the lane together. Ernie casually enters the Queen's yard without any hesitation.

"You see? They know me," he says, as he approaches the chickens. "Who do you think brought that poor, shy woman her groceries every week?"

"You did?"

"Yes, every Friday night. And I'd collect the rent at the same time. Did you know that the Queen — why do you kids call her that? — has rented this house from my family for sixty years? Before that, she lived on top of my grandfather's store, on Fairmount Street. Moved there when my father was a boy, in the twenties, and stayed until the war ended, in the mid-forties.

Did Ernie say Fairmount? Isn't that the street my grandmother told me she moved to, after her family was evicted from Dorion? If so, that means that she and the Queen have always lived on the same street. Well, ever since the Queen came to Canada. First Dorion, then Fairmount, then here on Querbes Street.

"Poor Karika," Ernie continues, "she never owned much. Did you know there is no word for 'own' in Karika's language? To gypsies, at least back then, owning didn't mean much. I always stopped to greet her chickens when I came," Ernie explains. The chickens do seem to know him. They are clucking around his feet, nudging him with their beaks as if to say hello.

"Is that why she moved here from Fairmount? Because she knew you?" I ask Ernie, stringing my questions together so quickly he must think I'm crazy.

"Knew me? No, I wasn't born yet when she moved here, but she knew my father. He owned this store before I did. It's in the blood you know, shopkeeping. Karika came into the store one day

and recognized him, and asked if he knew somewhere she could rent near here. My father had
bought this house — he originally intended to fix
it up — when he bought the store. So, he rented it
to Karika. She said she had family on the street. I
never did know who that was."

Family! The word catches in my throat like a
chicken bone. That could only mean one person
— my grandmother.

"Are you going to help, child?" Ernie asks, trying to get my attention. I nod, still unable to speak.

Ernie simply picks up the birds and puts them
in the box. They don't flinch or protest. I wonder
if my grandmother had such an easy time gather-
ing the Queen's birds all those years ago on
Dorion. It would have been hard for her to do
without attracting any attention, but maybe the
street was pretty empty by then.

Ernie picks up the chicken coop, which must be
actually lighter than it looks, and I follow him up
the lane, carrying the box of chickens. In Ernie's
yard, we set the coop up in a corner and then Ernie
goes inside to fetch a bag of birdseed from the
store.

"What did your wife say?" I ask when Ernie
comes back.

"Oh, well, she doesn't like it, but that's too bad.
My wife was never very sympathetic about
Karika. Her family never lived through adversity,
not like Karika's back in Europe. Spanish flu,
poverty, war! Did you know that if Karika hadn't

left Romania when she did, she might not have survived the Holocaust that came twenty years later? So many gypsies were killed! And, my people, too, of course." Ernie stops talking then and just stares at the ground for a few minutes, shaking his head. "My grandfather left Poland long before the war, and was the only member of his family who survived. Everyone who stayed behind eventually died … There are certain things some people can never understand. You and I will help look after the Queen's chickens for as long as they have left, eh? They're very old, you know?"

"How old? As old as her?" I ask.

Ernie laughs. "Maybe," he says. "She was a gypsy, after all, magic potions and all that, right?" I promise him I'll take on the responsibility of feeding the chickens every morning before school. He'll do the night shift.

I know my grandmother would approve.

Chapter 14

I spend Saturday morning researching gypsies again, for my project. I can't stop thinking about what Ernie said, that if the Queen hadn't come to Canada, she might have been killed in the concentration camps in Germany, like his grandfather's family. And it's probably true. I found out today that 500,000 gypsies were killed by the Nazis. They had to wear black triangles instead of the yellow stars the Jews had to wear. I wonder who the Queen left behind and whether they survived.

The other day, Ms. Melinowski said that if we wanted to, we could invite a family member to class to watch us present our family history. She said it would be really interesting to meet the people we were writing about, if they were still alive. Min is going to bring her grandfather, and he's going to read some of his poems, the ones that almost got him killed back in China.

I try to imagine myself leading the Queen of Sheba into the classroom. My classmates would flip.

I keep thinking about the Queen of Sheba at the hospital, all by herself, with no family to visit her. She must be concerned about her chickens, too. Unless Ernie has somehow told her what we did, she'll think they're still in her yard, starving to death. I don't know for sure whether the Queen was taken to the same hospital as my grandmother, but I find myself sitting on the 80 bus, speeding down Park Avenue to Pine. When I get to the Royal Victoria, I go to the reception desk to find out what room the Queen is in.

"Excuse me," I say. "I've come to visit a friend of mine. She was brought here on Wednesday. She's an old woman with long reddish-grey hair. Her first name's Karika, I don't know her second name."

The woman punches the name Karika into her computer and presses enter.

"Karika Mineshti?" I nod. There can't be more than one Karika here. "I have her listed here in room 412, fourth floor," the woman says in a deadpan voice. I can't help thinking that, if she knew more about Karika Mineshti, who she was and what she's been through, she would have sounded a bit more enthusiastic.

I find room 412 at the end of a long corridor. I stop outside the door, take a deep breath, and peek around the corner and see the Queen lying in her bed, which has been raised so that she's almost in a sitting position. On the table beside her sits a monitor exactly like the one my grandmother was attached to, drawing the same wavy green lines.

I tiptoe into the room, afraid of startling her. I wish I could do this without being seen, which is crazy. I can hardly talk to her without letting her see me, unless I stand on the other side of the curtain that surrounds her bed, and talk to her like some kind of shadow puppet.

When I'm about a foot from her bed, she turns her head toward me. Her gaze is steady and unsurprised, almost as though she's been expecting me. I look down at her hands, clutching the rim of her blanket. Her fingers are long and skinny, like straws, and her nails are still pointy but no longer red.

I keep moving closer until I'm standing against the railing of her bed. I'm closer to her now than we were that day in the Old Man Park. Her eyes have been following me the whole way.

"I … " I start to speak, then stop, unsure of what to say next. "I just wanted you to know …" The Queen's chin lifts up and down slowly, as if she's encouraging me.

"I wanted you to know that I saved your chickens. You don't have to worry about them. Ernie and I are looking after them. I'm helping to feed them. They'll be okay."

There! I said it. I feel like running out of the room now. But the Queen's presence has me glued to the spot. Suddenly, her hand starts to lift from the bed. I watch it rise slowly. I can see by the lines of concentration on her face that it's taking her a lot of effort to make this gesture. She raises her whole arm straight up in front of her. Then she swings it to the right, in my direction, like a crane. Her nails slice the air between us, stopping only inches from my face.

"*Thanks you, Elaine*," the Queen whispers, her voice very faint and raspy, as though it hasn't been used in a long time.

It doesn't matter that the Queen has called me by my grandmother's name. I raise my hand to meet hers. Our fingers touch. Her skin is as fragile and papery as an old leaf. She closes her fingers over mine. The pressure is gentle, like a baby's. I wonder if the Queen would tell me more about how my gran rescued her chickens back on Dorion. And how she ended up on Fairmount, too. I could go on pretending I'm Elaine, and maybe the story would come out, but I can't do it. And I guess it doesn't really matter anyway.

"You're welcome, Karika," I say. The Queen's eyes glisten when I say her name, shining with a strange kind of beauty.

Then her fingers release me and her arm falls back to her side. She closes her eyes and hangs her head, obviously exhausted. "*The Queen is ninety. No spring chicken!*" I remember my grandmother's words. The green lines of the monitor are waving across the screen. I imagine them flying off the screen and into the air, out the hospital window, and across the city to the port, then down the river to the Atlantic Ocean and all the way across to the country, town, and perhaps even the house or shack Karika was born in.

I recall the ritual I read about this morning. Karika would be wrapped in a red scarf, a red cap on her head, and a red amulet hanging around her neck. Her mother is smiling down at her, wearing a purple scarf over her head, with gold coins dangling from it onto her forehead, to show she's married. It's the seventh night of Karika's life. Her mother is trying hard to stay awake on this important night. This is the night that Karika's future will be determined by the Fates. I wonder if the Fates decided all of her future that night — the house on Dorion, my grandmother, Ernie's house on Querbes, right up to this moment, here in the hospital with me.

"Goodbye, Karika," I whisper, turning to leave.

I decide to walk home. The whole way up Park Avenue, I still feel the pressure of the Queen of Sheba's hand where it squeezed mine. Stalking the Queen was one of the main activities of my childhood. Today, holding her hand, I left all that behind. I keep looking at myself in storefront windows, to see if I look different. I feel like I should, somehow.

Before long, I see the first of two tunnels I'll have to walk under to get to my neighbourhood. It's already getting dark. It'll be supper by the time I get home. My mother must be wondering where I am.

I'm waiting for the light to change, looking around, when I see a door open on a dilapidated building across the street. A young girl steps out, followed by an older man. They both approach a waiting taxi. It's only when the girl looks up that I realize it's Cindy. I want to call out to her, but something about the way the man has his hand on her back, and the way her head is down, stops me. It's like she doesn't want to be seen. And what would I say anyway?

When the man gets a bit closer, I can see that it's Lorne London, the model scout. He looks different than he did at the mall. There, he was dressed kind of funky, in jeans and a hooded sweatshirt. He looked younger. He's in a suit today, with a leather jacket.

The taxi takes off, toward downtown. I walk up to the building and look at the signs beside the door, under the various buzzers. The one on the third floor catches my eye: *Agence de mannequins Belles Modèles Modelling Agency*. Cindy must be doing some jobs, just like Lorne London promised. I'm suddenly really curious. I'd kind of like to see where she's working. I open the door to the agency and step inside, into a dark stairwell. I practically have to feel my way up, along the wall. At the top, I push open a door. The office is just a small room with a large steel desk that holds a phone and a small stack of paper. A filing cabinet stands against the wall, under the window that looks out onto Park. Well, would look out if it wasn't so dirty. The walls are covered in framed pictures of models. I scan them, looking for Cindy.

I'm about to leave, when a door behind the desk opens and a man steps out.

"What can I do for you?" he asks. He's looking me up and down. When he smiles, two dimples sink into his cheeks. Maybe he's a male model. He looks like he could be on the cover of *GQ*.

"Oh, nothing. I was just wondering about modelling," I say, thinking fast. I guess I expected the place to be busy, and that I could just look around quickly without being seen, then leave.

"My name's Daniel," the man says, coming around the desk. He places a hand on my shoulder and stares intently at me. "So you want to model? You definitely have the looks. We have a lot of success with our girls here. We're always looking for fresh young faces." His hand is clutching my shoulder, like a claw. I don't know what to say. I try to catch a glimpse of myself in the dusty window, but it's too dark. I can't figure out what Daniel's seeing. Me, with modelling looks? I haven't washed my hair for three days and this morning I just pulled it back into a ponytail. Maybe it's my dark brown eyes — but the rest of me must be way too big and short.

"First we take some shots, work on your portfolio, your comp cards, put you on our website.

Do you want to try it?" He increases the pressure of his fingers. I remember Cindy bending into the taxi, Lorne London's hand on her back.

This is all moving way too fast.

"I'll think about it and come back, maybe with my friend," I say, backing up. "She wants to model, too."

"Don't wait too long. We have lots of work right now. I've been in this business a long time, and you have the looks, believe me."

"Okay, well, thanks," I say. Then I turn and leave, running down the dark stairs two at a time.

I'm surprised I don't break my neck.

Chapter 15

Every time I see Cindy at school, a picture of *Belles Modèles* pops into my head. I want to talk to her about it, but I never see her alone, so I don't get the chance. I'd also have to confess that I actually went up there to snoop on her. How would that make me look?

On Thursday, in English class, while listening to a tape of *The Merchant of Venice*, Cindy's hand slides out from under her chin and her head hits the table with a loud thwack. Our English teacher yells at her to wake up, but Cindy doesn't move.

"Penny, tap her on the shoulder for me, will you?" The way he says it reminds me of a game we used to play in kindergarten, where everyone would sit in a circle and we'd sing, *Take a little friend and tap her on the shoulder*, then run around chasing each other.

Why did he have to ask me?

I lean across the aisle and tap Cindy's shoulder. It's like there's no fat on her at all now, just skin stretched over bone, like the models in the pictures I saw at *Belles Modèles*. Cindy doesn't budge. I push her arm. It feels like a long fork, with a small hand stuck on the end. Still no response.

Her face is white and her eyes are slightly opened. I can see her pupils, but it's pretty clear she can't see me.

"Sir," I say over the tape. "I think something's wrong." Mr. Cheswick comes over, rolling his eyes. He's probably used to people passing out during Shakespeare, the way he teaches it.

He shakes Cindy's shoulder roughly. Her right arm slides off the table completely, dangling limply over the edge. We all gasp.

Someone in the back shouts out that she must be dead.

Mr. Cheswick pulls a cellphone out of his back pocket and makes two quick phone calls. A minute later, the principal shows up, and helps Mr. Cheswick lay Cindy down on the floor. I can't help thinking how disgusted Cindy would be to find herself lying on the dirty floor, which is littered with gum, eraser shavings, and old Kleenex.

Mr. Cheswick dismisses the class and tells us to go to the library. People stop to gawk at Cindy on the way out, just like cars slowing down beside an accident on the highway, causing a pileup near the door. Min, Sharon, and I are huddled together, staring down at Cindy's long, thin body, laid out on the floor. The school nurse is here too now, patting a wet cloth against Cindy's forehead. She seems to be waking up a bit and is rolling her head from side to side.

"Girls, to the library," Mr. Cheswick says, pointing. I want to argue, to tell him I should stay because I'm Cindy's best friend, but that would be lying. What can I do except leave along with everyone else?

We don't speak until we're tucked away at a back table, behind the stacks of books.

"Do you think she's going to be okay?" asks Min.

None of us has the nerve to say "I hope so" out loud. We're supposed to be mad at Cindy.

"She's been modelling," I tell them. "I saw her coming out of a place on Park Avenue on the weekend. She was with that scout we saw at the mall. I went up and looked around. It was a modelling agency."

"Maybe she's just working too much then," Min says. "Doing late-night shoots and stuff."

"Could be," I say. I remember the way that guy Daniel clamped his hand onto my shoulder. He was pretty forceful. He'd be hard to say no to.

"Serves her right," says Sharon, finally. She's been absolutely silent since she saw Cindy laid out on the floor. "I don't even care." I think Sharon enjoyed standing over Cindy, looking down on her for a change. But Min and I just look at each other. We know Sharon's right, in a way, but it's hard not to care at all.

***

Later that evening, sitting at my desk, I look out my bedroom window at Cindy's second-floor flat. I wonder what's happening up there. They must have called Cindy's mother to come get her at school. I don't think that's ever happened before. I stare over there on and off for a couple of hours as I'm working on the computer, but I don't see anyone go in or out. You'd think Jason would show up at least, to see if she's okay. Cindy never did invite people over to her place much. I can't imagine that her new friends, whoever they are, have been calling in. If she's too sick to go to school tomorrow, she'll just lie there all alone, all day. Her mother can't miss work easily, I know that. She used to ask my grandmother to pop round and check on Cindy when she had to stay home with a cold. If my grandmother were still alive, she'd be making her chicken soup or something. She'd also have noticed Cindy getting skinnier by the day.

I guess that's how *Belles Modèles* wanted her, how they'd want me if I'd gone through with Daniel's invitation.

I recall Cindy coming out of the agency with her scout, his hand on her back, as though he had to push her along. Why was she reluctant? Cindy's always wanted to be a big star. She should've been running to the taxi.

There's some part of this story that I just don't get.

I look up at Cindy's bedroom window again. We used to have signals — blind all the way down meant we couldn't play, halfway up meant call me. All the way up meant urgent — need to speak to you now! I know it's silly. We haven't done it in ages, but I tug my blind hard and send it springing to the top. Cindy's blind is down all the way, like she's shut herself off. As if she's not just across the street, but on the other side of a wide ocean.

I'd need a pretty big bridge to reach her now.

Chapter 16

On Saturday, my mother comes home from Ernie's and calls me to the kitchen.

"Guess what Ernie just told me?"

"What?"

"The Queen of Sheba died this morning."

I'm stunned for a few seconds, even though I shouldn't be. She looked so old and frail. It took all her effort to raise her arm and hold my hand at the hospital. And now she's dead. I guess she wanted to follow my grandmother one last time.

"That's too bad," I say, finally. I wish I could tell my mother about my visit to the Queen, but I don't feel like getting into it with her.

Later, I drop by Ernie's to feed the Queen's chickens. The animals are now round and plump. Ernie built a better coop, an insulated one that can help them survive our freezing winter. He figures it will be their last.

Ernie comes out back and tells me that the city wants to buy the Queen's house. "It was always a health hazard," he says. "I would have done it ages ago, but I didn't have the heart. My father promised her she could stay there as long as she needed to. The city's been after me for that property for ages. They want to build a park, in the spring."

I can't imagine kids playing on the Queen of Sheba's old property. The monkey bars will probably be built where her house now stands. Climbing on them would be like climbing the beams of the Queen's old house. The sandbox will cover the area where she kept her coops out back. The kids will be able to unearth old chicken bones if they dig deep enough.

I'm glad I'm too old for playgrounds.

Cindy didn't come to school yesterday. I watched her place on and off last night too, and I still haven't seen anyone come or go. Jason was at school and he didn't seem bothered about it. He was hanging around with his usual crowd, laughing, smoking, like he didn't have a care in the world.

I wonder what Cindy would say if she knew the Queen of Sheba was dead. She'd probably be glad. Cindy could never stand the sight of her or her crumbling house. I think of those high-rises Cindy wants to live in one day — new and shiny and perfect, all the things Cindy tries to be. All the things Lorne London has probably told her she could be. Except, what's perfect about getting so thin you don't have the energy to hold up your head?

I stop at the foot of Cindy's stairs on my way home from Ernie's. I wonder what she'd do if I knocked and asked to come in. And, if her mother answered, would she let me in? She might think I had something to do with Cindy's troubles. I don't know how much Cindy tells her. For all I know, she doesn't even know about the modelling.

I knock anyway. The worst either of them can do is slam the door in my face. But I won't know if I don't try.

Cindy's pale face appears behind the glass. She looks surprised, and reluctant to open up, but eventually she does.

"Hi Cindy."

"Hi." She looks around behind me, as though she doesn't trust who's out there. Like maybe I brought a film crew along, to capture her at her worst.

"Relax. It's just me. I was just wondering if you want to come for a walk."

"Why?"

"I don't know. You can't stay inside forever, can you?"

Cindy just shrugs. Then she reaches behind her for her coat.

"Okay," she says. "But I don't want any questions about what happened. I was just tired, that's all."

"Okay, I promise. No questions."

We stroll up the street toward the Queen of Sheba's house. Its middle sags even lower since the Queen's been gone, as though she had been the main beam holding it up.

"Did you know that the Queen of Sheba died this morning?" I ask.

"Really? No, I didn't know."

"Yeah. And I found out they're turning her house into a park."

"You're joking. Who's going to want to play in there?"

"That's exactly what I thought." But for different reasons, I think to myself. I just couldn't stop thinking about all the mean things we'd done to her.

We stop at the Queen's yard. Cindy runs her hand along the rickety picket fence. We used to believe we'd be electrocuted if we did that. Before I can stop myself, I'm opening the gate.

"What are you doing, Penny? I'm not going in there."

I start up the front stairs, remembering the last time I walked up here, how my legs were shaking. I press my nose to the glass and stare inside, but all I can see is darkness. When I press a bit harder, the door moves.

"Oh my God. I think it's unlocked." I turn the knob and push. To my amazement, it opens. The lock looks busted. I guess the ambulance technicians had to break it when they took her away. But nobody bothered to fix it.

"What should we do?" I turn to Cindy. "Do you think we should actually go inside?"

Cindy's still standing back at the gate. She shrugs. "I don't know."

"Remember you used to say it probably looked like the Haunted House at Laronde, full of spider webs and skeletons."

"We could just take a quick peek," Cindy says. She climbs up the stairs and stands behind me. I'm afraid that going inside the house will be invading the Queen's privacy, something my grandmother wouldn't approve of. But I think the Queen wouldn't mind too much, after what happened at the hospital. I'm not a complete stranger, after all. So I push the door.

The house is dark and musty, like it hasn't been cleaned in ages. I feel along the wall and flick up a switch. A weak hall light comes on, lighting up a room to the left. We tiptoe to the doorway and stare into a bedroom that contains a single bed covered in a patchwork quilt. A bureau beside it holds a brush, comb, and mirror set. A few tubes of lipstick and pots of makeup are scattered around. Even from the doorway we can see that some long reddish, gray hairs are clinging to the comb.

"Yuck," says Cindy. "She actually tried to make herself beautiful. Why would she bother?"

"Probably to try to look nice," I say.

"Are you serious?" Cindy rolls her eyes.

We continue down the hallway to the living

room. An old maroon sofa sits along the wall. Across from it is a rocking chair covered with another quilt. In between, there's a table covered with magazines, like *Vogue* and *Cosmopolitan*. Ernie must have slipped them in with her order. Cindy's staring at them with her eyes wide, like she can't believe the Queen would have beauty mags.

"Did you know the Queen of Sheba was a gypsy?" I ask.

"A gypsy?"

"Yeah. She was Roma. She came over here from Romania in 1920."

"How do you know?"

"My grandmother told me. They lived on the same street."

"In 1920?"

"Yeah, and forever after that, too. They were kind of … friends."

Cindy's mouth falls open but she doesn't say anything. We are shuffling down another hallway that probably leads to the kitchen. I feel for another light switch.

"Why didn't you ever tell me?" Cindy asks as I flick up the switch.

I'm about to answer her when my eyes are caught by the most amazing sight. Cindy must be as amazed as I am, because we both gasp at the same time. All along the wall of this tiny hallway are shelves. Sitting on the shelves are dozens, maybe even hundreds, of beautifully painted eggs. The shells are decorated with flowers, birds, vines, suns, moons, clouds, rivers, and waterfalls. Cindy and I just stand there, taking each one in, not knowing what to say.

"Did you know about these too?" Cindy asks.

"No way. I don't even think my grandmother knew about these. It's not like she ever came here."

"But why would someone want to make such beautiful things if no one was going to see them?" It's a good question. I picture the Queen bent over her eggs with a tiny paintbrush in her hand, working so carefully, choosing her colours as though they really mattered.

"Maybe she just loved making them. Maybe looking at them made her happy. It's not like she had anything else."

"But I could never do that," Cindy says. She sounds really upset.

"What?"

"Keep all this locked up and not show it off. I mean, that would be such a waste." Cindy's staring intently at the eggs, as if she's trying to understand it all. I have the feeling Cindy's not really talking about the Queen or the eggs, but about something much more personal. Something she's got to figure out.

"You mean like you, not modelling?" I ask. "At *Belles Modèles*."

Cindy's jaw drops again. "How did you know?"

"I saw you there, by accident. I was walking

home. I saw you come out with that model scout."

"Oh." Cindy studies her feet. She's really quiet. That bright edge she always had seems to be gone.

"Cindy, what happened?"

"I just couldn't keep up all of a sudden. Lorne said I needed to lose weight, if I really wanted to make it. He was helping me put my book together, but he said I'd have to pay for the pictures, a lot of money. And if I can't get work, I won't be able to afford them. My mother can't help me out."

"But is it worth it to you, to have to go through all that?"

"Well, yeah. I mean, if I don't have the modelling, what do I have?"

I'm thinking of something to say, to make her see that she has lots going for her. Her thin arms are wrapped tightly around her chest. It's true that, at the moment, it doesn't seem like she has much. Nothing but herself, and she's disappearing.

"You have Jason," I say. "You wanted him."

"I don't know, Penny. I think I've lost him. He said I was a wreck. It's so easy for you, Penny. You don't care what people think of you. And you have this perfect family and everything. I don't have that. All I've ever had is pretty. I thought I'd see my picture up in lights, that everyone would see it. Everyone was so impressed when I told them it was going to happen. People seemed to like me more."

"Not me. I liked you better before. Remember?"

"Yeah." Cindy doesn't say it out loud, but I bet she's thinking that I'm easy to impress. It's other people she wants to impress, people like Jason.

"Hey, we can't just leave these beautiful eggs here," I say finally. "They're going to demolish this house. They'll just all be broken."

"So what'll we do?"

"Let's at least take some of them. I don't think the Queen of Sheba — I mean Karika — would mind. Did I tell you I saw her in the hospital last week? She even held my hand."

Cindy's eyes widen. I think she's going to say something like "gross" but she doesn't. Before today, I'm sure she would have. But it's hard to associate the word "gross" with someone who could paint such fine and delicate details. If there's one thing Cindy responds to, it's beauty.

"Let's take that quilt off the rocking chair and put some eggs in it. We'll figure out what to do with them later."

We choose about twenty eggs each. We don't really have time to be too picky. Cindy's got to be back before her mother gets home from shopping. Poor Cindy. She's got no soft place to fall in that house. The eggs are lighter than I expected because they've been hollowed out. That also means they're more delicate.

"That was really neat, Penny," Cindy says, when we reach her front stairs. "What you told me about the Queen and everything. And what we saw."

"Yeah, it was."

I put my hand under the quilt to give the eggs extra support as I sneak them into my room. I lower the bundle carefully onto my bed.

Miraculously, not a single shell is cracked.

Chapter 17

On the way home from school on Wednesday, we all stop and take a good long look at the Queen's house. A dumpster is now sitting beside the curb. Over the top of the house we can see the tip of a small crane that must be sitting in the lane.

"We'll finally get to see the Queen's stuff," Sharon says. "I'm definitely watching."

"Yeah, well don't expect to see much," I respond. "She was really poor." The Queen's personal belongings probably won't even fill five boxes, like my grandmother's did.

"Well, you never know," Sharon says, offended.

Cindy and I look at each other. Neither one of us mentions the eggs. I'm afraid if I did, Sharon would want to go in and smash them all up or something. Besides, no one knows Cindy and I took that walk. Sometimes, you just need to keep secrets. This one isn't harming anyone.

Besides, I think finding those beautiful eggs, hidden away in this old house that everyone has always seen as an eyesore, somehow gave Cindy the courage to come back to school, even though she's not looking her best these days.

Things have been strained all week, because Cindy's been hanging out with us instead of Jason. Nobody knows what to say to her. That first day, at lunch, I tried to chit-chat away, to make it seem like nothing was unusual. But Sharon and Min were just confused.

Jason walked right by us a couple of times. I kept expecting Sharon to let out a big "ding," just to embarrass Cindy.

It'll take a while for things to get back to the way they were. If they ever do.

Later, we watch the large crane that holds the wrecking ball manoeuvre into place. I don't know why they need a wrecking ball. The house is so dilapidated someone could probably just jump on the roof to cave it in.

A police officer nudges us to the other side of the street, warning us to keep out of the way. Then a crew of men wearing work gloves, construction boots, and hard hats enters the Queen's house and begins carrying out her belongings. They form a kind of assembly line, passing out lamps, dishes, and clothes, which they throw into the container. The bed and bureau we saw yesterday, along with the sofa and rocking chair, eventually make their way through the assembly line. I think of what Ernie told me of the Roma language, and the lack of a word for "owning." It's true she didn't have much.

"Did you see them?" Cindy whispers to me.

"No, did you?"

She shakes her head. "Maybe they were in one of the boxes."

It's just so tragic to picture all the smashed, colourful bits of shell. But when we see the shelves being carried out, we know that must have been the eggs' fate. At least we rescued a few of them. I like to think that some of the workmen may have recognized how beautiful they were and put a few in their pockets to bring home.

The Queen's stove is the last thing to be carried out. Two men lift it high over the rim of the container and let it drop. Its two black burners stare up at us like black eyes from on top of the heap. The dreaded stove, where we all escaped being turned into chicken feed when we were kids. I can almost laugh now.

Then the crane, from which the big steel ball hangs, motors up. A minute later, the ball falls like an angry fist from the sky to crush the memory of the odd woman whose name hardly anybody knew.

"Wow!" exclaims Sharon. "What power. It's completely crushed." Sharon's obviously enjoying watching everything about the tall Queen shrink and diminish. "She's like nothing now."

I think about trying to convince Sharon that the Queen was never nothing, but what's the point?

When the men have all left, and the remains of the house have settled in a big heap, Adam and his friends dip under the yellow plastic tape to rummage through the rubble. They're like scavengers, looking for bits and pieces of the Queen's belongings. I want to shout at them to stop, but I guess that if I were still ten and didn't know the Queen's story, I'd be digging there too.

"I'm going to check it out," says Sharon. She bends under the tape, calling out, "You'll be sorry if I find something." The rest of us watch Sharon dig. She seems to be digging more fiercely than the others, as if she really believes the Queen might have had gold and jewels stashed away somewhere.

After a while the group of kids participating in the dig grows bigger. Kids are picking up pieces of brick and hurling them at the wreckage, as though they want to break it up even more. I notice Jason among them. He's lifting big pieces of wood and pumping his biceps with them, as if he's at a gym. Suddenly a chant starts up: *"Double double, toil and trouble, stinky queen's stinky rubble."* Both Sharon and Jason are singing it at the top of their lungs.

Cindy is cringing behind me. She doesn't want Jason to see her.

"I can't watch. I'm going home," I say. Cindy

kind of hides behind me until we are down the street, then she goes home too.

My mother is sitting in the kitchen chair my grandmother used to sit in, drinking a cup of tea. "What are you doing home?" she asks.

"I don't know. I don't feel well. I'm going to lie down."

"Guess what I just heard on the news?" my mother asks. "The old Park Avenue train station is going to be saved. It's going to be renovated and turned into a community centre. They're going to build the supermarket somewhere less historical."

"Wow, that's fantastic. Some people do respect old things, after all. Granny would be happy."

"You bet she would," my mother agrees. She's quiet for a minute, then she says, "Listen, Penelope. I didn't want to tell you before, because I wanted to wait a while, but I'd like you to go through Granny's things. There are some boxes in her room. I want you to take out anything at all that you want to keep. There are some neat old things in there. I've already taken what I want. The rest we'll send off to the Salvation Army, okay?"

"Okay." I can't tell her that I've already taken the souvenir tin. The Queen's old note is hidden away deep in my top drawer. My mother obviously doesn't know anything about it all. If my grandmother had wanted her to, she would have told her. The only reason I can figure for her secrecy is that she was respecting the Queen's privacy. Somehow, the secret seems much more powerful because of it.

"Mom?"

"Yes Penny."

"I was wondering … do you think we could go to the Queen's funeral, I mean, if we haven't missed it?" I hold myself tight, waiting for my mother's reaction.

"That would be a really nice gesture, Penny. I can't imagine who will arrange it. She doesn't have any family here. But the hospital must be making some arrangements. I'll call in the morning."

"Ernie might know," I say.

"Ernie? Why would he know?"

"Just because. They were closer than you think, Mom, trust me." My mother just looks at me, impressed.

"All right. If you say so."

I'm ecstatic. I know that it's completely right for someone from our family to attend the Queen's funeral.

"It's funny, isn't it, Penny? How the Queen of Sheba always followed your Granny?" my mother says.

"Yeah, it is." I can't believe my mother knows this. She's never mentioned it to me before.

"She once told me that, when she married my father, she just didn't feel complete until she let the Queen have her new address. She said it would have been like leaving without her shadow. I never really did understand it, but it was clear that she meant it."

So that was it, the final piece of the mystery. That was why the Queen left her apartment above Ernie's grandfather's shop on Fairmount, and followed my grandmother here.

"I wonder why she got called that?" I ask.

"I guess it's because she was exotic," my mother says. "Like the original Queen of Sheba in the Bible. She tested King Solomon's wisdom by asking him all kinds of tough questions and didn't give him any gold until she was satisfied with his answers."

"Wow, I didn't know that." What's more astonishing is that I didn't know my mother knew it. I guess I'll have to spend some time getting to know my mother. When my grandmother was around, I didn't have to. But that's changed now.

Along with so many other things.

Chapter 18

On the weekend, I start working on my history composition, which is due Monday. I've been putting off writing it for a long time, just because I haven't been sure I could actually do it. I'll have to read my story out loud to the whole class, and reveal that my grandmother was friends with the batty woman of the neighbourhood.

But once I start writing it, the story just flows. I put myself in young Karika's place, imagining myself all alone in Romania, living at the orphanage, my family dead. Coming to a strange country all alone on a boat, not knowing the language. It must have been awful. She must have felt like she had no one in the whole world who cared about her.

It takes me only two hours to piece the story together. And another two hours to put together the fact sheet on the Roma people and the Spanish flu and the Jacques Cartier Bridge. Then I find the pictures I want to use. I had most of those chosen already. The young dancing girl will go on my cover. I'm more and more sure that the Queen of Sheba would have looked just like her, before leaving Romania. I love the girl's expression, happy and carefree as she swirls. It's nice to think the Queen was once like that.

On Monday, when Ms. Melinowski calls my name, my heart beats wildly and my knees shake as I stand to read my story. My voice is weak at first, like I can't pull it up from my bone-dry throat, but as I read and get into it, my voice grows stronger. Before long, I forget that I am facing a room full of people who have always seen the Queen of Sheba as nothing more than a nutcase. That includes Min and Sharon. I know they're going to be shocked. They might even be angry that I knew all this and never told them.

But I just try to forget all that and read the story. I read it the way my grandmother would have wanted me to, as though I couldn't care less what anyone else thought.

Karika Mineshti, a ten-year-old girl, was staring out of the orphanage on the outskirts of Bucharest. The window was covered in cobwebs, blocking her view of the road below, where a horse-drawn carriage had just pulled up. Karika watched a woman step out. She was wearing a long skirt that swept the dust. Could she be coming for Karika? Karika imagined the rich home the woman lived in, its warm fires kept blazing by a young maid. Karika could be that young maid, if she was chosen. Being a maid would be hard, because Karika was used to being outdoors. She had always played in the fields, rivers, and trees. Being stuck in a big house, and wearing a stiff maid's uniform, instead of the long skirts and loose shirts that flowed around her as she ran, would be hard. But Karika would have no choice. That's because her own family — her father and mother, aunts, uncles, and three younger siblings — were all killed by the Spanish flu that was raging through Europe, killing thousands and thousands of people.

Karika heard her name. The matron was calling her. Could it be? Would she be going off to the big house in the city?

"This kind lady is willing to send you to Canada," the matron said. "There, a family will take you in and give you work."

Canada, Karika thought. Where was Canada? Was it over the Transylvanian Alps, or down the Danube River? Did she have to take a boat? Boats looked like fun. She'd seen them in the Black Sea, when she lived beside it with her family.

But the boat ride wasn't fun. It was horrible, from the minute the ship pulled out of Constanta, to the minute the voyage ended. Karika had a wooden board for a bed in the belly of the ship, where hundreds of people huddled. The trip lasted for days and days, as if they were sailing to the end of the world. Karika was sick the whole time. She thought maybe the Spanish flu had found her at last. She couldn't make it upstairs to be sick in the sea, so she used a bucket by her side, like so many other people did.

Finally, the ship was still. Karika could barely walk. Her legs were weak from lying down for so long. She didn't know where to go, so she followed the crowd, clutching her bag made of old carpet. At the bottom of the ramp, a nun put her hand on Karika's shoulder and led her away. She spent the night in a warm clean bed and ate hot soup, her first food in many days.

The next day she was delivered to a large family on a street called Dorion. Karika had never seen such a big city. There were cars everywhere and buildings so high they touched the clouds. The city, called Montreal, made Karika feel small. Only one thing made her happy in her new home — the little yellow chicks she kept in the backyard. She liked watching them grow into plump chickens. Every day they laid perfect eggs, which she used to cook the food for the eight children she had to care for. Little by little, she got used to her new life. She decorated her room, a cupboard off the kitchen, with colourful scarves. And she grew spices — chives, basil, and oregano — to make the food taste the way she remembered it.

Life went on, until one day the family told her they were leaving. The husband had no more work and they were going to live with relatives in the country. Karika longed to go to the country, too, to the mountains and streams, but she had to stay behind. They let her keep her chickens. Karika sold their eggs to make money. The children on the street came to her to buy eggs for their mothers. They played in her yard, jumping and laughing around the chickens. Sometimes she played with the children. Then she wrapped their eggs in newspaper and handed them over carefully.

One day she noticed boxes appearing on people's doorsteps. The children who came for eggs talked about having no money, and hunger, and having to leave. Then the police were at her door, telling her she had to leave, too. She thought she had done something wrong, but couldn't figure out what. It was just like the stories her parents always told. Her mother said Christians believed her people had made the nails that killed Christ, and so they had to pay. They weren't allowed in parks or public places, so they had to hide away in the woods, out of sight. Karika saw the mountain that sat in the middle of the city of Montreal and pictured herself living among the trees like the goddess Bibijaka, who lived in the forest and shone like gold.

The police then told her the bulldozers were coming to destroy all the houses on Dorion Street so that they could build a bridge over the Saint-Lawrence River. She was told to pack her boxes, so she did. The police carried her boxes into the backyard and covered them with plastic. The police came back, for her this time. They took her to a place called the Salvation Army, where she was treated kindly. But she missed her chickens and cried for them at night.

Until one day a little girl she recognized appeared at the Salvation Army. She had a box in her hands, and in it were two of Karika's beloved chickens, looking happy and well-fed. The little girl, Elaine, told Karika that she had taken the chickens with her when her family moved to their new street, Fairmount. She didn't know what to say, but she thanked the little girl in her poor English. A few days later, Karika took the box and walked many miles to Fairmount. There, she saw a "For Rent" sign above a butcher shop. She was afraid for her chickens, but didn't tell anyone she had them. Not right away. Only when she knew it was safe. Eventually, people came to her for fresh eggs, and the kind man who owned the store allowed her to keep coops out back. The son, a friendly young man, grew to love the chickens. Karika thought he might like her, too, but one day he married and moved away.

Karika watched Elaine, who lived down the street, grow into a lovely young woman. She didn't talk to her though. She kept herself separate from everyone and let her red hair grow long.

Many years later she got a note: "I'm glad you have done so well, Karika. I am getting married and will be moving to Querbes Street, near Saint

Roch. I wish you all the best. Your friend, Elaine."

So Karika travelled north in the city and found this street called Querbes. There, she was surprised to see the grocer's son, the one she used to like, who now had his own store, one like his father's, but bigger. She asked him if he knew a place she could rent and he showed her an old house he had bought. Karika loved it. It had a big yard with a beautiful maple tree. Her chickens thrived.

Karika carried on as usual, but went out less and less. She couldn't sell eggs, because everyone now bought their eggs at the corner store. So children didn't come into her new yard, just as they hadn't come into her last house either. All that had ended long ago, on Dorion. But she still dressed the same way she always had, in the long skirts and loose shirts her ancestors wore. She thought of changing, but decided not to. Her clothes made her feel closer to the people she'd left behind.

Then one day, the children began throwing stones. They chanted rude songs and held their noses when she passed. She went outside even less than before. Only once in a while, when she felt the walls of her house pressing her in, like a leaf between waxed paper. But she tried not to let it bother her. She concentrated on painting her eggs. She had learned the art back in Romania, from an old aunt. First, she tapped a tiny hole at either end of the egg. Then, she blew the egg out, keeping the shell intact. Next, she drew beautiful patterns into the egg with hot wax on the tip of a toothpick. Then she painted the rest of the egg. When the dried wax was peeled off, a design appeared. By the end of her life, Karika had painted over a thousand beautiful eggs.

This way, when she heard the kids calling her the Queen of Sheba, she stayed at peace inside. She could pretend she was still in Romania with her family, like the days before the fever hit and took everyone away from her.

Karika watched Elaine's daughter grow, and eventually her two grandchildren. She knew they were among the kids who persecuted her, but she forgave them. She knew that for centuries people had been following the crowd and joining in the meanness, even when they didn't know why. But Elaine continued to smile at her whenever she passed the old house, and this made Karika happy.

Until one day, another note arrived. "Dear Karika, My grandmother, Elaine O'Grady, has died. Her funeral will happen Saturday at the Houseman Funeral Home on Park Avenue at two o'clock. She will probably be buried near her husband at the Mount Royal Cemetery. Regards, Penelope, her granddaughter."

Karika snuck into the cemetery to pay her last respects to the one person who had always made her welcome in this new land. But, with her friend gone, Karika grew weak. She felt herself fading. She thought of her family, all dead, and how they *must be reincarnated by now. Maybe some of her chickens had carried the souls of her relatives over the years, and that's why she loved them so much. She wanted to be reincarnated that way, too, not as one of the living dead, seeking revenge on anyone who'd harmed her. She preferred to think of Elaine's kindness and forget the rest.*

When a young girl who looked like Elaine came to her hospital bed, and held her hand and spoke her name one more time, Karika felt happy. When this girl told her her chickens had been rescued again, she sighed with relief. Her face glowed with a strange kind of beauty. A beauty that came from the woods and fields of Romania. A beauty that couldn't be wiped out by all the insults of the New World.

No matter how hard we all tried.

The entire room is silent when I finish reading. Ms. Melinowski, who doesn't live in our neighbourhood, looks confused. There had been so much clapping for the presentations before mine, especially for Min's story of her grandfather. When he read his poems, most of us had no clue what he was saying, but he read them with such emotion, we couldn't help being moved. Min's translations into English didn't even make them better.

But I guessed this would happen. I knew people would be surprised and wouldn't know how to react. I had planned for it. So, before the silence grows too large, I pull out my shoebox of painted eggs. I brought one for each member of the class.

"I'd like each of you to have one of the Queen of Sheba's eggs," I say. "I think you'll be amazed by them." I hope Cindy doesn't mind. Technically, half of these should be hers. But she sends me an encouraging smile.

Min and Sharon both give me a strange look when they choose their eggs from the box. Sharon seems almost afraid to touch it, as though it might explode.

There are now ten eggs left. I want to put one on my grandmother's grave, and one on the Queen of Sheba's when we go to her funeral on Saturday. In the end, Ernie decided his grandfather would have expected him to help the Queen have a proper burial, so he's paying for the funeral. It'll be pretty low-key. I'm going to see if the other members of the Queen of Sheba hit squad will come, once I've explained more about the whole business, and convinced them that I haven't always known all this. It's not like I've been a jerk for years, throwing stones at the Queen's house and picturing her playing with my grandmother at the same time. I could never have done that.

I can't be sure my classmates will treasure the eggs. Some of them may simply crush them into their pockets, or whip them across the tables in the cafeteria at lunch. But I can't control that, and I guess in the end, it doesn't really matter. The point is that everyone in my class now knows more about the Queen of Sheba.

Now they know that what they saw on the outside — her weird clothes, wrinkled skin, and freaky red hair — was not the whole story. There was so much more to her, including her beautiful eggs, hidden deep inside the broken-down house.

I think she'd like that.

Chapter 19

This time, it's not a freak snowstorm. It's the real thing. The sky is dark grey and the snow is falling fast. We've been watching it from our classroom windows all afternoon, and by the time we leave, we are actually walking in a couple of inches of powder.

I'm kind of glad, because the falling snow is creating a kind of curtain between me and my friends.

"If it snows all night they might cancel school tomorrow," Sharon says.

"They never cancel school for snow," Min says. And she's right. We're always hearing about school closures in other parts of North America, especially in the southern United States, where everything shuts down when a few inches of snow falls. Here, the only time school closed was for the ice storm a few years ago, when the entire province was encased in three solid inches of ice that knocked out power and basically crippled the city for weeks.

Speaking of ice, I feel like I have a few inches of it to get through right here.

"Listen guys," I say. "That stuff about the Queen of Sheba. I didn't know any of it before a few weeks ago, I swear. My grandmother never said a word, not once."

"But I can't believe you kept it to yourself, even when you did find out. I don't get it," says Sharon.

"Yeah. Why didn't you tell us anything?" asks Min.

"'Cause I was still figuring it all out. I didn't even know that I could do the story until the last minute."

Cindy's walking with us. She's looking better these days. She's not starving herself at least. She says she told her mother everything, and her mother suggested she save the money her father sends her for a few years. That way, when she's a bit older, she can try modelling again if she wants to, and she'll have money for the photographs and stuff. Her mother called Lorne London and told him to back off, and that he had no business recruiting girls our age and pushing them the way he did, especially without contacting their parents first.

"You know how my mom gets," Cindy told me. "I don't think I'll be seeing him again. It was pretty cool though, listening to her tell him off."

"Hey guys, remember this post?" I stop beside a hydro pole that is one of many running along the back lane between our street and school.

"Oh my God, check if there's anything inside," says Sharon.

I stick my hand into the hole. That's what we used to love about this pole. For some reason, it has a deep hole in it, a few feet up from the ground. It's like some dumb squirrels thought it was a tree. We used to leave notes for each other in it. We called it our private postal service. No stamps needed.

"There won't be anything in there, Sharon," says Cindy. I hold my breath, hoping Cindy won't tell Sharon to grow up. Sharon has barely said a word to Cindy since she came back to us.

"I'll check," I say. I stick my hand into the deep hole, scooping out the bit of snow that has already collected there. "It's empty."

"Hey, we could put something new inside," says Cindy. "Want to Sharon?" Cindy has never asked for Sharon's approval before. Sharon looks bewildered.

"Okay."

Cindy dumps her knapsack in the snow and finds a piece of paper. "What'll we write?"

We all stare at each other. No one wants to make the first suggestion.

"It should be something really meaningful," says Min. "To do with what's happening right now, with us." Sharon and Cindy nod. They must be thinking about the fact that we're all back together.

But then Cindy says, "I mean, it should be about the Queen of Sheba." That's exactly what I wanted, but I didn't dare suggest it. Min and Sharon still seem prickly about my hiding things about her from them.

Cindy's about to write something. But then she hands the paper and pen over to Sharon. "You do the writing," she says. "Your writing is way nicer than mine."

"I know what it should say," I say. "It should be really simple. How about 'The Queen of Sheba hit squad was here, November 2nd, 2000'?"

"But add that we're not that any more," says Min.

"Say 'The former Queen of Sheba hit squad,'" says Cindy.

Sharon writes the sentence, folds the paper up as small as she can, then shoves it way to the back of the hole in the pole.

"Now what?" says Sharon.

"Maybe someone will find it there in twenty or thirty years and wonder who the hell the Queen of Sheba was, and why she had a hit squad," says Min.

"They'll think she was a drug dealer or something," says Sharon.

"Or a real queen," says Cindy.

We continue up the lane. It's always really pretty when the snow first falls, before it turns to slush on the ground. It coats the bushes and tree limbs, and covers up the grey of all the tin back sheds. When we get to Ernie's, I stop.

"I have something to show you guys," I say. When I turn into Ernie's yard, walking right up the Rat House, my friends all gasp.

"Penny? What now? Are you going to tell us Ernie is your grandfather or something?"

"No, come and see." I wait until my friends are in Ernie's yard with me, then I go around the shed to the coop that Ernie built. It's kind of a two-storey thing, with two birds on each floor.

"The Queen's chickens," I say, holding out my hand.

"How did they get here?" asks Sharon. "I just assumed they died, or got taken away by the police or something."

"I asked Ernie to help me rescue them."

"You mean that part of the story was true?" Min asks.

"It was all true. Well, mostly. I had to make some things up. Here, help me feed them," I say, pouring a handful of bird seed into each of my friend's hands. "It's fun. They're sort of cute, once you get to know them." I throw some seeds in the snow and open the hatches. Only two jump out.

"Are there any other secrets that you're going to spring on us?" asks Min.

Cindy and I look at each other. Only she knows where I got the painted eggs. I remember standing in the dim light of the Queen's hallway, hearing the house creak, as though the Queen was still walking around. The eggs were so colourful, they lit the place up. It's like Cindy and I were standing in another time and place, staring at the eggs. As far as I know, we were the only people apart from the Queen to ever lay eyes on them.

Cindy is waiting to hear what I'll say. I know the moment was magic for her, too.

I won't spoil it by telling.